A
LOADED
GUN

STUART HUTCHINSON

A Loaded Gun
Published by The Conrad Press in the United Kingdom 2015

Tel: +44(0)1227 472 874
www.theconradpress.co.uk
info@theconradpress.co.uk

ISBN 978-1-78301-852-9

Cover and book design by:
Charlotte Mouncey, www.bookstyle.co.uk

Printed by Management Books 2000 Limited
36 Western Road
Oxford
OX1 4LG

For Dorothy

My Life had stood – A Loaded Gun –
Emily Dickinson
Poem 754

I

Grabbing a handful of his hair through the hood, one of the men yanked him off the chair.

'C'mon, Captain Portway.'

Was it day or night? Inside the thick black hood he'd been in darkness for nearly all of two days; ever since they grabbed him on the fourteenth of February from his rented house in King's Street Canterbury.

Fourteenth of February, 1984; a Valentine's Day he'd never forget.

Lying peacefully in his bed in the evening in Pat's arms, after they'd celebrated the day together, he'd wondered if this could be love; wondered if, doing what he did, he could ever expect to find love, let alone peace.

For five months, ever since they'd met in Brighton in October, Pat had been so caring, so convincing; right up to that moment in Canterbury when Pat's three comrades ran up the stairs, burst into the bedroom, and one of them, pushing an automatic pistol into his face, said, 'Wake-up call, Captain Portway.'

Forcing him into some clothes, they'd hustled him down the stairs and onto the street, straight through the rear door of a Land Rover, waiting immediately before his house, its wheels on the narrow pavement, its engine running, a girl ready to drive off. Inside the Land Rover they hooded him, as they pushed him down between the bench seats, his head towards the windscreen, their feet stamping on him as they sat above him.

For about two hours they'd driven - where? Then he was pulled out of the Land Rover to be marched across gravel into another house, where his wrists were manacled to his feet, and he was beaten unconscious, till he came round, and the beatings began again, and again.

One of his captors knew how and where to hit, all right. Under the hood his nose was broken, his teeth smashed, his mouth nearly always full of blood. Some ribs were cracked. Any movement, any cough, was a bayonet into his chest, stabbing him again, now, as he fell from the chair onto his hands and knees, and the man pulled his head up, stretching his neck, holding him like a dog.

I'm going to die *now*, he thought, as the man wrenched his head still higher. The IRA are going to kill me. It's me for the O'Kanes.

As soon as they'd manacled him, his captors had briefly snatched off his hood to show him half of a torn photograph, another copy of the same photograph that had been pushed mysteriously through the letter-box of his Canterbury house, as soon as he had moved in last December. The photo showed the handcuffed Paul and James O'Kane helpless in his custody, slumped exhausted against a Saracen personnel carrier in South Tyrone in March 1981. They were what was left of an IRA killing squad ambushed and wiped out by British soldiers. Portway didn't need any photo to remember the huge wound in Paul O'Kane's shoulder, or the raw bruises on both their faces caused by the soldiers smashing them about. Two of these soldiers had force-marched the O'Kanes over to him - passing the parcel, till the music stopped for the O'Kanes, when he delivered them for interrogation to a Loyalist splinter unit, and they disappeared forever.

Who took the photo, his side or theirs, or somebody working both sides, Portway never knew. Maybe it was whoever warned the IRA team there'd be an ambush on that South Tyrone afternoon. But why wait nearly three years after 1981 to push the photo through his letter box, and was it a warning or threat? Always, it seemed, the past had you in its grip, even when, as a lone agent assigned to MI5, you believed your fate might be in your own hands. Instead, it was always as much in somebody else's - Pat's this time.

He'd heard Pat's voice while he'd been hooded, though he was sure Pat had played no part in the beatings.

'Up you get,' the man twisting his hair commanded, pulling him to his feet and dragging him into a stumbling walk. His shoulder banging against what must be a door- frame, Portway was suddenly outside, in a frost as fierce as when they brought him here. He heard gravel crunch underfoot again, and then, as a big door slammed behind him on what sounded like a heavy latch, he knew he was in another building not as warm as the house. Kicks to his shins and ankles and a shove on his back pitched him onto plastic sheeting, the man still holding his hair, wrenching his head to one side.

'You're still not going to give us anything?'

It was the voice of the woman who'd been the driver. He'd glimpsed her when they snatched off the hood. She was dark-haired, petite, pretty; in her twenties, like himself and the other men he'd seen.

'What were you searching for in Brighton, before you followed us to Kent?' she persisted.

'You're going to kill me anyway.'

'You know we have to, if only for Paul and James O'Kane. But why not confess?'

'Fucking get on with it, if you've got the balls.'

'Balls are no problem,' she said.

Hands round his neck rammed his face into the sheeting, as other hands snatched up the hood and bared his head from the back, so the muzzle could bore straight into the side of his skull, behind his right ear.

'I can't give you absolution,' the woman said, 'but here's your OBE.'

He was a boy again, in one of the army houses; his father at the head of the table, explaining the honours system; his mother clearing away the dishes. They'd search for him, because they loved him, loved each other.

'OBE, Guy,' his father said, 'Order of the British Empire, awarded to civilians.'

OBE, father, one behind the ear, was the last thought of his life.

II

In the six months he'd known her, Steve was getting to like the way Helena changed his routines.

This sunny Sunday morning in March, for instance, here he was driving with her from Canterbury in his Jaguar sports car for a walk along the Kent coast - Deal to St Margaret's Bay and back.

Before he met Helena, Sunday mornings had been his regular time for a run, especially since leaving the parachute regiment after tours in Northern Ireland and then the Falklands campaign. All his life he'd been determined to stay fit. Even when United said they weren't renewing the three-year contract they'd given him straight after his O levels when he was sixteen, he knew they'd no complaints about the shape he was in. Like everybody else they were only amazed he quit football at nineteen to sign on as a Para. After the army ten to fifteen miles on a Sunday morning cleaned out the week he'd had; tuned him up for the next one; kept him in control.

But that was before Helena.

Not that she was against running. Smiling at her as she adjusted the passenger seat to lie back and listen to classical music on Radio Three, he remembered they were together because of it.

It had all begun last year, September 1983, which was always going to be a big month for him, because it was the month he started as the new director of Canterbury University's sports centre. Then, ten days in, it became an even bigger month, when Helena walked into the sports centre to enrol and happened to find him alone behind the refurbished reception counter, checking for faults in the joinery. Very matter of fact, she'd asked where she might find a running partner for the dark autumn and winter evenings: 'Another woman perhaps?'

Hardly hearing the question, he'd been captured immediately by the by the directness of her eyes, which seemed as if they'd never had to look away from anything. While he searched for an answer to make a connection with her, she bent forward to fill in the membership form and write out her cheque, his gaze uncontrollably following the curve of her breasts into her V-neck sweater beneath her soft wine-red leather jacket, and the wisps of brown hair escaping an elaborate silver clasp and curling down the back of her neck. Later she told him the clasp was 'a Victorian comb, very pre-Raphaelite; a present from an aunt,' but in the brief moments at the counter he knew instantly he would love to be so intimate with this woman that it would give her pleasure to let him release her hair from it. A glance at the form she slid back to him revealed her to be an academic in the English department. In the year he'd already done as an assistant at the sports centre he'd hardly exchanged twenty continuous words with a female academic. Would a woman like this ever be interested in him?

'Well, there was a woman runner working in the library,' he said eventually. 'She left during this summer. I'm not sure I know any others.'

But then, accepting her cheque as she shrugged, he risked instinctively, 'I could be available, if you're not too pacey.'

Offering his hand he added more confidently as she responded with hers, 'I'm Steve Wilson by the way; in my first weeks as the sports centre's new director after just over a year as an assistant. Meteoric promotion, you might say. I'm the enforcer for all the new regulations and charges!'

He was trying to be a bit jokey, but sensing she wasn't following him, he went on: 'There's been big changes all over the campus, start-date this month, September eighty-three. Every department's got to make money and pay its way. The sports centre didn't use to charge any staff or students. You didn't even need to enrol. The old director didn't agree with the changes, so he's been paid off, and I'm in his shoes.'

'You mean I'm too late for all the freebies!' she exclaimed. 'Just my luck!'

He grinned, 'How long have you been here?'

'Ten days, still finding my way around. I'm Helena Edwards, by the way, a one-year appointment in English. Thanks for your offer about the running. I'll think about it.'

'No problem. My number's in this year's new internal directory.'

'Mine's not. I was appointed too late. It's causing me all sorts of hassle.'

A week later she phoned him in his office to arrange their first five miles.

At twenty-seven, about three years younger than him, and four or five inches shorter than his six foot one, she thrilled him by soon matching his fitness, her lighter speedier stride keeping pace with his larger heavier one on runs stretching eventually to ten miles.

Then there was the first time they spent the night together at his house - a small, rented, brand new starter home, just off Canterbury's Whitstable Road. It was after a late afternoon run in October, after he cooked his first meal for her, a lasagne she was amazed to see him layer together himself.

'That was lovely,' she murmured, as they both lay in his bed, returning to consciousness.

'I hope there'll be more,' he sighed, caressing again her smooth heated body and gently kissing her full breasts, her closed eyelids. Already he was sure making love to her was a sensation he would never have enough of, because he'd never felt so fulfilled. Immediately he'd sensed her pleasure beginning from her trust in him, and his own confidence growing from that trust. Never before had sex for him been so mutual. No other woman had wanted to please him as much as he wanted to please her.

'I didn't think anyone bearing the title "director" could be so fit and powerfully muscled,' he could still hear her, half-teasing him, as they lay together that first time, her palm resting on his six-pack. 'Aren't directors supposed to be fat and middle-aged?'

Now in March, driving into the bright sun on their way to Deal, they'd been together for nearly six months. He hadn't said much to her about his United experience, just telling her how, after leaving the army, he'd come to Canterbury from Atherstone, his home town ten miles west of Manchester; how it was all because of the Jag, and his best mate Yatesy.

'Talk about muscles,' he said to her, 'wait till you see Yatesy. He's a body-builder.'

This was part of telling her how he and Yatesy had left the army in July '82, after the Falklands, him with no idea what to do, where to go; Yatesy to move in with Carol, his childhood sweetheart, and also to join his father in a car breakers and repairers, and general demolition business based in Canterbury's Wincheap area.

Steve explained how he'd had a phone call in Atherstone from Yatesy.

'It's me,' Yatesy had said, when Steve picked up the phone. 'How about buying the car of your dreams?'

'Which car of my dreams?'

'A Jaguar XJS V12, and no, I'm not kidding. I've had this yuppie wanker in the yard nearly all morning. He's smashed up the wing of his Jag and he's no money to fix it, even at our prices. He's ready to be shut of it quick, so I thought of you, mi old misery.'

'What's it like?'

'Three years old and "pristine", as we say in the trade; silver, with cream leather and blue piping. Fix the wing, at a special price to you, you're quids in. Spend some of that money you didn't booze away. Didn't you always say this was your dream motor?'

Coming down to Canterbury in August '82 to buy the car, Steve saw the ad for an assistant at the university sports centre. 'Everything must have been leading to you,' he told Helena.

But where was everything leading now, six months on? What did the relationship mean for Helena? He knew what being with her meant for him. She took him out of himself and made him very happy in a way no woman had ever done before. They ran together and had great times in bed. He cooked for her, because she never cooked for herself; fixed her Renault Five and the sagging book shelves in her flat in St Augustine's Road – but was all this enough for her? With her widowed father an Oxford professor of history, her own first degree from Oxford and then PhD from Cambridge on an American poet called Emily Dickinson, this woman relaxing by his side in the Jag's passenger seat came from worlds he knew nothing about. He was proud to be with her, but was sure her colleagues questioned why she was with him.

'Don't think about our relationship too much,' she'd declared, sensing his doubts. It was during a fast lunch-time four miles, both of them well wrapped up against the December cold. 'And *don't*, for God's sake, think southern so-called intellectual middle-class girl and northern working-class rough.'

Letting him take this in while they pushed themselves hard up a short, frosted steep slope, she continued, hardly panting, after they'd reached the top, 'Just let our relationship happen - please. We'll find out where we're at if we ever get there.' Then, as they stopped to open a gate to cross a field, 'I'm just glad you're so confident in your own maleness. Men can drive you mad always wanting to know if it's ever been as good with anyone else.'

Leaving him to drop the loop of rope over the gate to hold it closed, and to wonder how confident he really was, she suddenly sped off, yelling back over her shoulder as he chased her, 'In fact you're anything but rough, and no, it's never been as good with anyone else - so much for my politics!'

She meant her membership of the Labour Party and him voting for Mrs Thatcher earlier that year in Maggie's '83 landslide - difference enough! But she'd also been to Greenham Common in the April before the election, holding hands in the human chain from Greenham Common to Aldermaston and Burgfield, protesting against American cruise missiles and their nuclear warheads. And the weekend before that fast December run she'd camped again at Greenham Common with her new friend Jan Woodhouse, an older, divorced, chain-smoking lecturer in Politics. He remembered spending that weekend alone, frustrated and gloomy, downing too much beer on his sofa, insisting to himself, 'Helena thinks the right words can sort anything. Nobody ever need be your enemy. She should try standing at the wrong end in a football crowd among the other lot's supporters.'

And now this March, to beat it all, when he still needed to be sure of where he was with her, there was her support for the miners' strike, and especially for the miners of Snowdown Colliery in Kent, a pit threatened with immediate closure. As soon as Arthur Scargill called the strike, she'd volunteered with Jan to shake a supporters' collecting tin on Saturdays, standing in the Longmarket in the centre of Canterbury, sometimes getting two-fingers instead of coins, and one man, about forty, mouthing to her, 'You need a good shag'.

'Politicians and their tough choices!' she mocked, returning to Steve's house the day before this drive to Deal, to eat and spend the night after the latest of these encounters, and responding to a Conservative minister on TV. 'It's never tough for them, only for people on the front line. Mrs Thatcher's a super-matron for the men in her cabinet. To women like me she's a nightmare. She wants to smash nearly everything I believe in!'

Why didn't Helena realise that having a woman leader like Maggie was strange for him too, he'd asked himself, as he broke some eggs into a mixing bowl to make tomato and cheese omelettes. Any team he'd played on, any pack of men he'd been with, the leader was never a woman. He hadn't had a woman class teacher since junior school, and after he left his boys' grammar school it had been footballers and Paras, even more swinging dicks.

He voted for Maggie's Tory party because she'd sorted the Falklands, and he'd helped her do it, for Christ's sake; helped her too in Northern Ireland! He wanted to stay on her side, because he might need her to stay on his.

Suddenly, out of nowhere, two photos of Paul and James O'Kane had been all over the media; one photo in their rugby kit, the other standing with their priest. The IRA was claiming the O'Kanes had absolutely disappeared in March 1981, because they'd been handed over to a British special agent after an ambush, and the agent had passed them on to a protestant murder squad.

Yatesy, panicking a bit and sinking two pints one straight after the other, had met Steve in the Bishop's Finger a week before the drive to Deal.

'What do we do?' Yatesy asked, after bringing his third pint from the bar and showing Steve the photograph in *The Sun* of the O'Kanes and their priest.

Neither of them had ever forgotten the vicious fire-fight in South Tyrone; a planned ambush of an IRA killing unit dropping the British soldiers in deep shit, because the IRA unit had been tipped off; three British soldiers dead; one of these little Roy Lewis on his first tour; always standing close to Yatesy, as if Yatesy's huge body would guarantee him protection.

'These two are special,' the sergeant had said to Steve and Yatesy, gesturing at what was left of the IRA unit, after five of them were killed, and everything was under control. 'Get them over to that captain who's just turned up in that Saracen.' No reports, nothing - as if the captain and the two prisoners they now knew were Paul and James O'Kane had never existed.

'You want to stay alive, don't you?' Steve answered Yatesy in the Bishop's Finger. 'So do and say nothing. Keep quiet, and people will be wrapping their fish and chips in that photo tomorrow.'

'I lost it, when we captured these two,' Yatesy said, indicating the photo and taking a huge swig of his third pint. 'Put my boot into them both; twisted the arm of him with the shoulder wound. It was because of little Roy - head blown apart, brains spilled out. I'd never seen anything like that before.'

'You weren't the only one who lost it. I had to pull you all off the prisoners, remember! That sergeant would have let you all go mad. He took a swing at the prisoners himself.'

That was an example of the front line, and Helena knew nothing about it; nothing about the miners, like his brother-in-law up in Atherstone. The miners were sure to lose, poor bastards, because Maggie couldn't let them win - them nor the Argies. Maggie knew about front line all right.

'It'll always be tough, you know, for a lot of people,' he'd answered Helena yesterday evening, sliding the first well filled omelette onto her plate, then pushing the salad bowl nearer to her. 'My mother's brother, Uncle Fred, lives three streets away from us in Atherstone, the town we all come from. He's never really been anywhere else, apart from fighting Mussolini and Hitler all the way up the leg of Italy to the Po Valley. One bloodbath after another he told me, three hundred thousand killed, wounded and missing. He's worked in a factory in the town ever since; nine hours a day on his feet at a metal stamping machine. He can't sleep now for the ringing in his ears, so he has a separate bedroom from auntie Annie. You have to look at him when you speak to him so he can lip read.'

Helping herself to salad, Helena didn't respond, and he didn't say, 'To keep you in your freedom, workers have to give up a lot of theirs,' because he didn't want to hurt her. He felt even Labour leaders lived in Helena's world and didn't want workers to be too demanding. That's why they couldn't lay a glove on Mrs T. They didn't believe what they said, because they didn't live what they said.

But later, last night, in his bed, relishing again the deep mysterious musk of her perfume as they lay wrapped around each other, all his tensions vanished, and he was sure any of hers did too. This morning, as soon as he opened his eyes, she kissed him and said, 'C'mon. There's a bright March sun out there. No running today. Let's enjoy a walk on the coast - Deal to St Margaret's Bay and back, pub lunch on me.'

They had breakfast and showered, Helena having soon appreciated the efficiency of what she called his 'minimalist soldier's quarters;' everything working, not like the jumble of her flat, where you stood under the shower and hardly got wet. Afterwards they slid into his Jag, not so efficient, and where most of his money had gone. According to Helena he listened to its sounds, 'as intently as other people listen to Miles Davis or to a late Beethoven quartet.'

Fair enough, though he'd never heard any Beethoven quartet and wasn't sure who Miles Davis was.

He loved the Jag, loved the surge of power when you floored the pedal, like now on the last empty stretch from Sandwich to Deal.

III

'You know Julius Caesar landed here in Walmer?' Helena said.

Deal, where they'd parked, was already behind them, and they were now walking in the sunshine, hands deep in pockets, along the path separating Walmer's gently sloping shingle beach from the open green space that ran alongside the town's main street.

'Beaches and battles,' she continued. 'My father's brother was killed in the Normandy landings. I wonder if as much blood was spilled here in 55BC as in the Falklands.'

Steve gazed at scarred fishing boats, slumped into the shingle, knackered. He tried to imagine Romans running through the sea into a battle.

'If it's hand to hand, cutting and thrusting, you've blood all over you,' he said.

Tell her, if she really wants to know, he thought.

'All over you, my God!' Helena exclaimed.

'Mount Longdon and Wireless Ridge above Stanley were bayonet charges through tracer fire. Frenzied killing. You chop into them anywhere to stay alive yourself. Me and Yatesy back to back in an Argy dugout.'

'Horrible!'

'Then there's the bodies, like litter. Prisoners. The Argies sent out kids. Some of them were crying. They were the same age as me when I left school to sign on for United.'

She moved close to him, offering him the comfort of putting his arm around her. They were passing Walmer's ivy covered castle, its ancient cannons targeted on the sea.

'One of the fundamental divisions,' she said.

'What?'

'Between those who've killed their fellow human beings, and those who haven't. Shakespeare's intrigued by soldiers. Iago speaks of the "trade of war" and killing in his first words to Othello, as if it's like any other necessary occupation.'

'It's necessary all right, Shakespeare or no Shakespeare. But I'm telling you, you can't know about killing till you've done it, and then there's nothing to know. You're just standing over a dead man who could be standing over you.'

She fell silent, till she said, 'I'm sorry, bringing Shakespeare up like that. You must think I'm all books.'

When he said nothing, she insisted, 'I do know something about the dirty double-dealing real world, you know.'

'I bet you do.'

'Suppose I told you I've become convinced my father's best friend is in MI5.'

'Suppose you did,' he responded, tightening his arm around her, as if playing his part in a game.

'I was at boarding school with his daughter,' Helena went on. 'She dropped all sorts of hints about him, when we were in the sixth form. I've lost contact with her now.'

'What happened to her? From what you've told me about that boarding school I thought you all went to university.'

'Not Beatrice Furlow - that's her name. She was a bit of a rebel. She's married now to the millionaire pop music producer Simon Gallagher. She's all over the newspapers and television. You must have come across her.'

'I'm impressed.'

'Oh, Steve, I don't expect you to be by *her*! God, this has come out all wrong. OK. Look at the situation I'm in here at the university. They employed me saying "permanent lectureship next year", because they knew I'd a chance of going to the States and might turn them down. But now they have me, they won't talk to me about next year. How's that for a double-cross?'

'Tough, no question. But you can't tell me anything about the university. I'm getting four grand less than the previous director. My pay cut's paying for his leaving package.'

Parting from her, he kicked a piece of shingle off the path back onto the beach, exclaiming, as much to himself as to her, 'The university has me by the balls.'

Then, turning back to her and aware of her slight alarm, he asked, 'Where will you go, if they don't sign you up again?'

'Depends what comes up on the jobs market.' Looking away from him out to sea, she added, as if it was something she didn't want to say to him, 'It might have to be the States - Colorado, if they're still interested in me.'

Jesus, he thought, as they began to climb the Downs. Where will it leave her and me if she goes to America? As if searching for an answer, he gazed at the Channel beneath them, seeing it shine in huge patches of silver where the sunlight caught it. From this height and distance ferries and other ships were slow silent toys.

'Let's have some escapism,' Helena suddenly announced.

He smiled back at her, 'Such as?'

'How about James Bond?' She produced a laugh, deep in her chest. 'I bet you don't know that the famous digits 007 were originally the number of the Dover to London bus.'

'You're kidding.'

I'm not. And here's something else. In *Moonraker* Bond has a dangerous adventure here on these cliffs with a beautiful girl and protectively takes her to St Margaret's Bay, just like you with me.'

'C'mon, Helena.'

'It's true. Read *Moonraker*.'

While he took this in she continued, 'Now that my thesis on Emily Dickinson is with a publisher, I've thought of starting on a book about how writers use real places, something I've always been interested in as a kind of hobby. In St Margaret's, I'll show you where Fleming lived.'

'Kent and Sussex are a goldmine for writers and places,' she continued. Dickens is all over Kent, and you've obviously got Chaucer and Canterbury, though there's no conclusive evidence Chaucer ever came to the city. Anyway heaps of other writers did - some you might not expect, like Herman Melville and Karl Marx; some you might, like Jane Austen, whose brother lived nearby at Godmersham. Somerset Maughan went to King's School and lived in Whitstable. Conrad lived in various places in Kent and is buried in Canterbury.'

Though he often couldn't follow her, he loved her passion for literature. It came off her physically, like a sexy arousal.

As they completed the climb, she exclaimed, 'Evelyn Waugh trained as a marine on these very Downs, and as for Dover, more or less everybody was there and said something about it - Gibbon, for example, and George Eliot, and Auden.'

'You've really gone into it,' he said. 'Let's hope the uni keeps you here.'

'Well, that's something I'm leading up to. I'm talking to the English Department here about setting up a research unit in "Literature and Place", beginning with all the data I've collected.'

'What are your chances?'

'Who knows? I've only just started here. I've no influence. But let's not be too gloomy.'

Reaching her hands to his shoulders, she turned him round to face the way they'd come. 'Look at that view!'

Forcing his mind away from thinking about their future he gazed with her towards Walmer and Deal, and the long curve of Sandwich Bay. With its Margate and Dreamland fun fair, he knew East Kent had its mini-Blackpool. But it struck him again how undeveloped and unconnected this coast could seem; as if all the life he'd grown up with in industrial Lancashire was in another country. To leave a town behind by simply walking out of it, like today, was always unusual for him. Where he came from towns ran into one another along roads lined with houses. Grim, but even to a loner like him there was solidarity in mass living. If you were up against it, so was nearly everybody else.

Now they were high and alone on top of the Downs, standing between the empty coastguard station and the war memorial, a tower of granite blocks commemorating sailors from 1914-19 and then from 1939-45.

Two memorials for the price of one, Steve thought.

Helena unzipped her dark blue hooded waterproof coat, part of her expensive walking gear. She gave it to him, while she pulled her sweater over her head, his eyes following the thrust of her breasts. Handing the sweater to him to stuff into his rucksack, and putting her coat back on, she went closer to the tower and spoke aloud part of the first inscription: '*TO THE GLORY OF GOD AND IN EVERLASTING REMEMBRANCE OF THE DOVER PATROL 1914-19.*'

Then round the side; again she spoke the words aloud: '*THIS STONE WAS LAID BY HRH ARTHUR OF CONNAUGHT KG. 19TH NOVEMBER 1919. AND THE MEMORIAL WAS UNVEILED BY HRH THE PRINCE OF WALES KG. 27TH JULY 1921.*'

'God, royalty, heroes, and patriotism,' she commented. 'Even if we wanted to, we can't unite these things nowadays, except perhaps in America, and there they haven't got royalty, though they always claim they have God. Did it bother you that some of us were embarrassed by the celebrations after the Falklands?' Before he could answer, she added, as if she still hadn't got over it, 'Winning that war saved Thatcher.'

'Don't tell me you wanted us to lose,' he countered, as if she couldn't be serious. 'Women at Greenham Common, you know, stack up a lot of support for Mrs Thatcher.'

As they walked on with no response coming from her, he added, 'Helena, listen. I was glad how it turned out in the Falklands, but I was more glad I was back in one piece. If I'd been killed, it wouldn't have meant anything to me to have my name carved in stone. It must help some relatives, but my mother's very down to earth about things like that. She's spent a lot of her life trying not to be fooled. And my dad knows the score. He fought in North Africa under Montgomery. Anyway his lungs are so knackered from smoking he can hardly walk across a room.'

'I'm very glad you came back whole,' she now said, taking his hand and squeezing it, and reaching up to him to kiss his cheek softly. Often she was tender with him, more than any other woman he'd been with. Like a blessing he never thought he'd have.

Eventually they were descending through St Margaret's, Helena saying, 'You can see why people live here. It's a kind of Mediterranean haven.'

'Costing a lot of money,' he replied, gesturing at the marine residences.

On the beach they turned in the opposite direction from the pub, so she could show him Fleming's house. Grey-white cliffs rearing immediately behind it, the house was almost in the sea.

'Fleming actually took the house over from Noel Coward, who lived here for about six years,' Helena said. 'I've been reading Coward's diaries about the period.'

As they gazed at the house, she commented, 'Thank God the arts, and the theatre especially, have always been accommodating to gay men and women.'

Steve didn't respond. Off and on they'd talked about changing attitudes to gender and sex, Steve never having discussed these issues with anyone before. He'd told her about men in the army and in football dressing rooms, seeing women only as prey, something to screw; and lads repressing gayness, terrified of being called 'a fucking fairy!'

And he'd told her about Maurice Sims, 'Simsy', whose funeral he would be going to. Simsy had been in the parachute regiment ten years before Steve. Who knew what kind of contact was Simsy searching for?

Successful head of sales at a local Mercedes franchise, and father of three girls, Simsy had shot himself through the heart three weeks ago, while sitting before his wife in his house in Canterbury. He'd used a German pistol his father had brought back from the Second World War. The inquest was still searching for any psychiatric history.

A week before the suicide Steve had had his last game of squash with Simsy, who was a fanatical user of the sports centre. To beat him you had to play to your absolute limit.

Afterwards, as they stood together alone in the sports centre showers, Simsy had suddenly revealed he'd been involved in 'Bloody Sunday' in the Bogside in nineteen seventy-two, while Steve was still with United. He'd been one of the soldiers firing into the civil rights protesters.

'Me and you,' he continued, his eyes closed against the world, as the warm shower and shampoo washed over him; 'we've been there. We know what it's all about; what has to be done.'

'Yeah?' Steve remembered muttering in response.

Now, taking firm hold of Helena's hand, he said, 'Let's get to the pub.'

Turning back to walk along the beach they faced a great white cliff descending into the sea. A huge car ferry was about to disappear behind it.

'On its way into Dover,' he said.

'From France, probably,' Helena replied. Then, entwining her fingers with his, she said, '"Ah, love, let us be true / To one another."'

'What's that?'

'"Dover Beach", by Matthew Arnold, the best lines in the poem.' Turning her face towards him to kiss him again, she said, 'I've always wanted to say them to someone.'

IV

Scrambled eggs, sausages, bacon, toast, butter, marmalade, pot of tea - sullenly making Liam's breakfast on a late March morning in a tiny cottage in the Kent village of Wye, Theresa found her thoughts again returning to the isolated farmhouse on the Romney Marsh. Again she was replaying to herself the shooting of Captain Guy Portway, her first direct kill.

'Which of you is going to shoot the prisoner?' Liam had asked. His slight, wiry body almost hidden in the easy chair in the lounge of the farmhouse, he was stroking his beard with one hand, holding the gun by its barrel with the other, and slowly waving it before them, as if casting a spell. Hooded and chained, and occasionally groaning from pain, Captain Portway was slumped on a straight chair in the kitchen.

Theresa always knew this moment would come as a test. None of them, except Liam, had ever shot anyone. Sean and Matthew were Semtex specialists. Pat was still stuck with recces, though he'd Judas-kissed the captain.

'He's mine,' she answered Liam, gripping the pistol's butt, so that for a second or two she and Liam were joined together, till he opened his hand, letting the weapon slip out of his palm.

Like he slides out of me, she thought.

She already knew she could do a recce, be a lookout, deliver explosives; but could she put a loaded gun to a man's head and squeeze the trigger?

In the farm house on the Romney Marsh she discovered she could, because she did.

Manacled and hooded, the captain knelt there on the plastic sheet in the barn; alive, tense, both of them waiting for it. Then he was knocked over like an animal in a slaughterhouse; his life gone - somewhere, nowhere.

I can do anything, she insisted to herself afterwards, every day.

'Six feet under,' Liam commanded, eyeing the corpse, his hand again on his beard; 'so his people never know what happened to him.'

Sean and Matthew, both of them big and running to fat, began stripping the body, but Pat wouldn't touch it. Small of frame, always pale, his ginger hair shaved close as if in self-punishment, he stood looking on, seeming as detached as a priest. Theresa saw his hands, hanging by his side, come together before his waist, so that the tip of every finger, as if seeking comfort, could gently touch its opposite. Then Pat turned to retreat to the house.

'And orders are it'll be six foot under for any of you,' Liam threatened his retreating back, 'if you say anything to anyone about this, or the photograph of Portway and the O'Kanes. British army, RUC, MI5, Special Branch, Scotland Yard - we keep them all up their own arses and one another's. Already the Labour Party's shouting at Mrs Thatcher for an inquiry into the O'Kanes. We'll have them all at each other like ferrets in a sack.'

Returning from the burial Sean and Matthew cursed 'that fucking frost' and began warming themselves at the iron stove in the farmhouse kitchen, where she'd burned the plastic sheeting, the clothes, the wallet and everything in it, watching the photographs curl up and shrivel in the flames: the one of Portway and the O'Kanes, and two other photos: Portway as a boy with his father, both of them kneeling and triumphantly saluting on a beach, each side of a wonderful sandcastle with towers and flags, and battlements guarded by toy soldiers; the other of the same boy and presumably his mother, both standing astride their bikes, smiles on their faces. What happened to the rings, the watch, and the gun was down to Liam.

'One more for the never to be resurrection,' Liam said to her bleakly when she was finished at the stove. It was as if he wanted her to reassure him that everyone would eventually step up out of their graves, or arise from their ashes, and be happy.

Already she despised the despair seeping out of him.

This unit was so small-time. She'd killed Portway, but he was buried as a mystery, as if it had never happened. She wanted big-time, like the Harrods bombing last December - world-wide attention.

But Liam took the official IRA line about Harrods. Independent, unauthorised operations like that, 'Fucked everything up. No British government would negotiate with an organisation having units out of control.'

'Orders to deal with Portway came right from the top,' he insisted to her again, when they were back in the cottage in Wye, after the killing, fifteen miles away, in the house on the Romney Marsh. He meant not just eliminating Portway, but also attracting the captain away from Brighton to East Kent last November.

'You want a mission? We have one,' he'd said to eight months ago, last August, in the flat in Brighton, where the IRA had sent her to join him.

They were to make sure the captain was on to them. Get him to follow them away from Brighton to Kent. No why. Just do it. Imperative the captain wasn't left sniffing around Brighton.

They were told the captain was gay, which was perfect for Pat who, pretending he was ready to become an informer, picked the captain up in October, in a pub in Brighton's famous Lanes, and soon told him the cell was about to move to East Kent, 'For something big.'

Then, Theresa remembered, there was the extra development. Everybody being set up in Kent, and Pat and the captain in a relationship, Liam went to London and returned with the photo: Paul and James O'Kane, slumped beaten and handcuffed against

29

an armoured vehicle by the side of Captain Guy Portway; handed into his custody, never to be seen again.

'It's extra special now,' Liam said, showing the photograph to Sean, Matthew and Pat at a meeting in the cottage in Wye. 'We capture this Portway, take him to a property on the Romney Marsh, work him over, and kill him. Give him something of what the Prods gave Paul and James O'Kane, when Portway handed them over.'

'He's on his own,' Theresa recollected Pat saying, as if strangely pleading for the captain. 'I think he's given up on his own lot.'

'Be sure you're not giving up on us,' Liam told him. 'You know the consequences.' Then, as if to twist the knife into Pat, 'We're going to grab him while you're in bed with him in his house in Canterbury.'

So they gave Portway a nightmare - rousing him from his sleep by Pat's side, hooding and chaining him, then driving him to the farmhouse to be killed and buried beneath sheep grazing forever.

No matter how much Matthew, who'd been a heavyweight boxer, hit Portway, he told them nothing about what he was doing in Brighton, or who actually murdered the O'Kanes.

February then, March now, Theresa reminded herself, thinking, every day, what next? Laying out Liam's breakfast on the small table in the cottage's cramped kitchen, and spitting into the scrambled eggs, she shouted up the stairs, 'It's ready.'

Canterbury and Dover barracks were military targets enough, but if she had her way she'd go for the cathedral, a castle, a country house; break their National Trust hearts. Make the British public know the price you had to pay for nothing you wanted.

'Bomb Canterbury cathedral!' Liam yelled into her face last night. 'After the Luftwaffe missed it, day and night! You're out of your mind. Christ, the whole country would go insane.'

He kept on at her as she moved away from him to the open staircase. Standing on the bottom step she was taller than him, their height no longer about equal. On there she wasn't what he called 'My little curly-haired five foot jockey.'

'Hit a military target or a pub with twenty-five dead,' he said, 'they'll get over it and talk to you. Destroy their heritage; forget any hope of a deal.'

As he calmed down, it was as if he was again making it clear to himself.

'With the British it's not religion. They have no real beliefs and can't understand anybody who has. They're bastards to deal with because they know they're right without ever asking themselves why. But they always need something to go and see, or look at on the telly; all that Queen Mother, Westminster Abbey, parading down the Mall - their *Antiques Roadshow*. Deprive them of that, I'm telling you, they'll really be murderous. There'd be open season on Nationalists.'

Striking miners must believe in something, she thought, when she was alone in the bedroom, before immediately wondering if you could have too much belief.

Standing with her back to the sink this morning, and drinking her mug of tea ('cup and saucer for me,' Liam insisted), she coldly watched him relish his breakfast, as if their life together in this cottage was settled for good. 'Maddie, Maddie, Maddie,' he sighed to her in bed last night, exciting himself with the name she used with Rick McKnight, the MI5 man; clinging to her like a baby.

'Remember, it's work with McKnight not pleasure,' he warned her again afterwards, lying on his back and drawing on a cigarette as if it promised salvation. Then he was again lamenting, 'Our own psychopaths and criminals, and the endless deceit of the British.'

Nearly forty, he'd been on the streets in Belfast in the sixties when peaceful protests were clubbed into retreat by the RUC and Protestant mobs. Shouting 'Catholic scum,' British soldiers had raided his family's house in the middle of a wintry night, smashing in the front door, tipping his mother and father, his brothers and sisters and him out of their beds; making his mother and sisters sit terrified and shivering on the bare kitchen floor in their night-dresses.

Last night he'd told her about his best friend at school, when they were both fifteen; how the friend was snatched from a dark street, taken to waste land and bludgeoned to death with scaffolding poles.

'When we found his body we carried it to his mother's and lowered it onto the floor. Three years later I was in Rome, looking at Christ's lifeless body in Caravaggio's *Deposition*.'

You're all self-indulgence, she thought, finishing her mug of tea; believing you're more educated than the rest of us, because you were training to be a priest. But you're just another man in my power, like Rick McKnight; talking about yourself, pleading for understanding, as if you're in bed with the Virgin Mary. You don't get it. Outside the Catholic Church a woman is equal to any man. She's free and in control. There's no submitting to your father, like a little girl; no litter of kids, because there's always abortion paid for by the IRA, just twenty-four hours in a luxury London clinic.

His breakfast concluded, Liam left her to clear the table and wash up, telling her again as he lit his cigarette and let his eyes assess her body, 'You need more than a mug of tea in the morning. What are you, seven, eight stone - not much to get hold of?'

'How much more is there of you?' she challenged, rattling his cup, saucer and plates into the washing up bowl. 'If there's any jockey around here, I'm looking at him.'

He knew she was taking the train from Wye later that morning to meet Pat at Ramsgate station. Pat was coming from his cottage in Faversham, where he had a part-time job stacking shelves in a supermarket, and from Ramsgate they were travelling to Deal further down the coast to check out the Marines School of Music as a possible target. Since killing Portway she'd been uneasy about Pat, who was twenty-five, and three years older than herself. How involved had Pat been with Portway? What did he think of her, Portway's killer?

Towards ten o'clock her train was passing through Canterbury West Station on its way to Ramsgate. Glimpsing the tower of the cathedral, she remembered standing a week ago before the site of Becket's tomb, and eavesdropping on a woman, two or three feet away, who was reading a description of the dazzling jewels and gold that used to cover the original shrine. A tall, powerfully built stud of a man, with hair as black as Theresa's own was listening patiently to the woman, but catching Theresa's eyes he rolled his own. There's a man to be equal to body and soul, Theresa remembered thinking.

That evening she'd mentioned Becket to Liam. She was wondering when a killing could be called an assassination.

'Canterbury must be glad Becket was topped in its cathedral,' Liam responded grimly. 'It's guaranteed tourists forever.'

V

Sitting in the crowded pew, Steve felt Helena's firm thigh pressed against his. He watched one of Simsy's sports centre mates place a hand on the coffin, look up towards the vaulted church roof as if he could see the sky, and declare, 'Simsy will be soon up there, competing on the squash ladder, running personal best times, and celebrating sixty-six!' In the pulpit the vicar smiled encouragingly, while Simsy's wife and daughters in the front pew were crying their eyes out.

'Ridiculous,' Helena said, as they emerged from the gathering in the church hall into the April sunshine. Walking to the car they saw the grave diggers in the church yard smoothing out the top of the new grave.

'Ridiculous? What?' Steve asked.

'All that stuff about Maurice Sims carrying on running and playing squash. He's dead. He shot himself through the heart. He's gone forever, except in people's memories - like my mother. She taught English in schools, but she's not teaching pupils in some fanciful heaven, looking down on my father and me, and waiting for us to join her. And what's sixty-six?'

'Nineteen sixty-six. When we won the world cup - Bobby Moore, Bobby Charlton, Geoff Hurst's hat-trick. We beat Germany four two at Wembley!'

Not sure if this was making any sense to her, he suggested, 'Simsy's mate was only trying to make people feel comfortable.'

'Why should we turn to delusion for that?'

'People just want to believe something.'

Helena shrugged, as if this was beyond her.

In the car she said, 'Do you believe in some kind of heaven - paradise? I mean, Steve, when you were bringing in bodies in the

Falklands and arranging them in rows, "ours" and "theirs", as you told me, did you think they were on their way to somewhere else?'

Putting the key in the ignition it was his turn to shrug. 'I don't know what I thought.'

'We just go back to the elements after we die,' Helena insisted, as he started the car and revved the engine for re-assurance. 'Neuroscientists with the most sophisticated equipment can't find the self, let alone the soul. There's only the physical body and brain matter, which is also physical. There's no absolute core. Emily Dickinson knew that. That's why her poetry's all about disintegration.'

But with her mention of 'brain matter' he was straight back to Northern Ireland, missing the rest of what she said. He was seeing the stuff that seeped through his fingers when he tried to hold little Roy Lewis's ginger head together, after it was smashed in the fire fight when they captured the O'Kanes. Then he had to pull Yatesy and some others off the O'Kanes.

'And that's it,' he said, half of him still in South Tyrone, half of him with her.

'That's it,' she replied, gently covering his left hand on the steering wheel with her own warm right hand, so that he was now completely with her again, where he always wanted to be. 'But don't despair. We can do something on the way, contribute, have a good time, have - sustaining relationships.'

Sustaining relationships, he thought, even if you leave for America. But all he said was, 'Contribute?'

She too thought for a moment before replying, 'Whatever sense there is in life, we make it - even if we don't always make a good job of it.'

'Make the world a better place, you mean?'

'Try to, if only in a small way - like you cooking for Yatesy, Carol and me this evening. We'll all be happier for it.'

He managed a smile, 'Let's hope so.'

He wished there was some motorway to drive on, somewhere to release himself and floor the accelerator, keeping an eye out for cops. Proving you were tuned up and equal to the car's speed was always exciting. 'What else is this Jag for?' he countered, when Helena protested.

But they were on their way from north Canterbury to Restore, the reclamations business Joe Yates and his partner Carol had recently opened in the village of Pett Bottom, a few miles south of Canterbury, so Steve knew they would be stopping and starting around Rheims Way and up the Old Dover Road, with only Nackington Road offering any chance of a driving thrill before the country road to Pett Bottom itself.

The original car breakers and demolition firm Yatesy returned to after the Falklands had been split up, Yatesy taking the demolition side, his dad looking after the car breaking yard till it could be sold off, and he and his wife could retire to Spain. What was now called Restore used to be a farmer's small holding, but for the last month it had become a business selling materials and fittings from the buildings Yatesy and his workers demolished.

'All kinds of people are looking to make their houses more interesting,' Carol had told Steve, when he came down to Canterbury to buy the Jag in August 1982 and met her for the first time, 'and there are shops in London we can supply for Islington trendies. We'll have all kinds of brass fittings, kitchen-ware, light fixtures, doors, fire-places, stained glass; original stuff you can only get when older buildings are knocked down.'

He'd sensed straight away he was hearing plans already delivered to Yatesy, as Carol imagined their life of self-improvement. She was a woman with golden curly hair, her lovely body honed by aerobics and now, as if to welcome the spring and the opening of the new business, visibly pregnant. One of three girls and a dad living off his 'bad back,' Steve knew she'd managed all the secretaries in the Canterbury office of a national insurance company. He also knew Yatesy was very proud of her skills, telling Steve Carol was top of his class at school. When Steve first met her, he saw that that with Yatesy, who was into body-building, muscling beside her she'd tackle anything. Catching her perfume as he kissed her on that first occasion, he felt a sudden envy of his friend and the directions opening up for him. Yatesy and Carol were seizing opportunities, creating better possibilities for themselves, and, Steve thought, you could do a lot worse than sleep with Carol every night.

Steve knew that in the army Yatesy had found himself, putting behind him the years of crime his father had been involved in the 1940s and 50s, when his father had come home from the war and drifted into an East End criminal gang. The original car breakers business was the gang's reward to Yatesy's father for saying nothing during an eight year stretch after a major bullion robbery in which Yatesy's older brother had been killed.

'Cars and stuff still come down to the breakers yard from London, needing to disappear,' Yatesy had told Steve in the army, as if there were ways of the world you just had to accept.

Amid these recollections Steve had been driving automatically, blind to the countryside. Now they'd reached Restore, and he swung the car through the big open gates into the parking area. As they walked through the yard to the barn, where Steve knew the tiny office was, they mingled with customers looking at materials kept in the open, Helena immediately taking an interest in some ornate, wrought iron garden urns. Steve saw Yatesy helping a bloke load a van with a Victorian fireplace, and then Yatesy turned to a young couple tying oak floorboards onto a roof rack. The mother was panicking, looking for her child. 'He's there,' Yatesy said, as if he couldn't wait to be a father. 'He's sitting on that lavatory pan, pretending to use it. I've been keeping an eye on him.' Arriving at the office, Helene and Steve found Carol behind the till and taking phone calls. To Steve she looked even more pregnant than when he last saw her a week ago. It was Helena's first visit to Restore.

'Carol, love, congratulations! You've a gold-mine here,' Steve said to her, wary of her bump as he kissed her.

'Sometimes I think it's already becoming a monster,' Carol replied, happily accepting Helena's kiss. 'It gives us no rest. From the minute we open it's either the phone, or people wandering about the place.'

'I bet it's lovely when everyone's gone,' Helena said, 'so peaceful. What a setting, surrounded by orchards, and so near the city. Walk to the top of the Downs, you can see the cathedral.'

'If only there weren't so much paperwork every night,' Carol sighed. 'But we're going to employ some more help during the day. I'll do nothing but the books. That's all I'll be able to do when the baby's here.'

'You'll do very well to do that,' Helena said. 'All the research shows working women take on tremendous burdens when they also have children.'

'Joe does his share,' Carol said.

'Yeah, Yatesy will be great changing nappies,' Steve joked. 'And to be a kid with all this space to play in!'

He couldn't help remembering the grimy backyards of his own childhood, and the terraced streets with a great cotton-mill (now derelict) at one end and the main road at the other. Was that, he wondered, why he hardly knew anything about nature, like the names of birds and flowers and trees? But lads he'd gone around with knew all about birds and could find nests, no problem. Helena could too. He'd just want to enjoy a walk for the exercise, and she'd keep stopping, like the other day: 'Look,' she'd whispered, 'there's a gold-crest, Britain's smallest bird. It's a cock, very fierce. It'll fight to the death over a hen in the breeding season.'

Yatesy was now shepherding customers away, making it clear it was closing time. Steve saw he held a powerful padlock and a heavy chain hung across his shoulders like an ammunition belt. They were to secure the yard gates when everyone was gone.

Steve and Helena were staying for an evening meal Steve was going to cook. It had been arranged when Yatesy was at the sports centre doing his weights programme the previous weekend. He'd run into Steve and invited Helena and him over to Restore to celebrate its opening.

'Lovely,' Steve said immediately. 'Helena's looking forward to seeing your new place. Why not get some salmon from one of your mates in Whitstable? I'll cook. It'll give Carol a rest.'

Among the four of them it was accepted Carol and he were the cooks.

'That'll be a real treat for Carol,' Yatesy said, giving Steve a soft friendly blow on the chest.

'Who taught you?' Carol had asked Steve, when he first did a meal for her and Yatesy.

'My sister-in-law,' he told her. 'When I was living with my mother and dad after the Falklands, she invited me over for a meal that I had to help to prepare. She'd recognised I was bored out of my skull. After that she gave me regular lessons and some books.'

Now, in the kitchen of the farm cottage that was part of the site of Restore, Yatesy had a whole salmon waiting for him.

'My mate in Whitstable said it wasn't worth cutting one up for me,' Yatesy explained. 'We can freeze the rest.'

They'd left the two women the barn, where Carol was giving Helena a tour of its contents. Now the women joined the men, Helena looking thrilled. She was carrying half a dozen tiles.

'These are very William de Morgan,' she exclaimed, displaying the strange bird designs. 'He worked with William Morris, you know.'

'It's like they come from somewhere in the East,' Carol said, tracing the designs with her finger.

'William de Morgan also wrote novels,' Helena added. 'One of them has scenes set in Herne Bay here in Kent. Towards the end of his life he became more known for his novels, even in America, than ever he'd been for his ceramics and stained glass.'

'Even I've heard of William Morris, but this other William's new to me,' Yatesy said from the stove, where Steve had ordered him to look after the spuds and other veg. 'I've no idea where the tiles came from. One of the lads must have brought them in.'

'I remember pricing them up,' Carol said. 'I'd never seen anything like them before.'

'I'm sure they're on special offer today,' Yatesy replied, giving Carol a big wink.

'We're nearly ready,' Steve called out, bringing the salmon from under the grill. 'Just the sauce to make with these lovely juices.' He meant the juices collected on the foil on which he'd grilled the salmon.

They were eating at the bare pine table which was the centre of the roomy kitchen. When everything was ready, Carol helped Steve serve the salmon and the sauce, then place the new potatoes, green beans, and carrots on the table for people to help themselves. Yatesy poured everybody a glass of Chardonnay, explaining that it was from a wine club he'd just joined. As they both came to sit down, Carol kissed Steve on his cheek, saying, 'It's like a birthday present to have a meal cooked for me.'

Plans to extend the cottage were lying at one end of the table, and as they ate, they looked at them, Helena being especially impressed by how sympathetic to the original building the extensions would be.

'Any matching bricks, Kent peg tiles, we need. They'll come my way for next to nothing,' Yatesy said.

You and Carol are on your way, Steve thought again: your business, your house, your baby. Helena and me?

'No grub like this on the Falklands,' Yatesy exclaimed, 'nothing like this beautiful sauce. Let's give Stevey a toast.'

As they all happily clinked their glasses, he said to Steve, 'How did you get on in your interview for that degree up in London?'

He was referring to a brand new part-time degree in 'Leisure Management', beginning next year in London, with special entrance arrangements for mature students. Steve had been interviewed for it a week ago, immediately after making an inquiry. They were promising to accept him on his O levels and his life experience; just go up to London for two evenings a week.

Sipping her wine, Helena said, 'I'm all for Steve doing a degree, though from what he now tells me about this new department I'm not so sure they know what they're up to. But he needs qualifications to make him less vulnerable, even if my qualifications leave me completely vulnerable at Canterbury.'

Do we want to go into all this now, Steve wondered, re-assured that the salmon was perfect. Best say something.

'The university up there, near Waterloo, isn't like the university in Canterbury,' he came in; 'more like office blocks. The professor who interviewed me had only just been appointed himself. He's from the hospitality industry, hotels mostly. He said I'd probably know more about leisure management than most of his staff. They've no experience of what I've got on my hands - all the grants I'm applying for, the money I'm borrowing, for the new all-weather playing surfaces, new fitness suite, new coffee bar.'

'I bet I know more about business than they do,' Yatesy boasted, smiling lovingly at Carol.

What's a degree to me, Steve was thinking. Because Helena's prospects at Canterbury were uncertain, she was already contacting the university in Colorado that had sounded her out a year ago. He couldn't begin to imagine living without her.

'Who would have thought Stevey and me would have come back to anything like this?' Yatesy now asked, helping himself to more of everything. Raising his glass in Steve's direction, he went on, 'But for Corporal Stevey in Northern Ireland and the Falklands, I might never have come back at all.'

He gestured to the ceiling with his knife, and Steve saw Helena look up as if she expected to see something. 'And when it wasn't Stevey, it was somebody up there deciding whether you lived or died, simple as that. In the Falklands especially in-coming rounds might as well hit you as anybody else.'

Carol put her hand on his arm and gave it a comforting squeeze.

Be careful what you say, Steve was thinking, giving Yatesy a warning look. Two nights ago Yatesy had been on the phone to him after an extended news item about the O'Kanes on BBC TV.

'You did more than OK,' he said to Yatesy. 'You never let anybody down, and especially in the Falklands.'

'Yeah, but when we were lying in that wet grass at Goose Green, after we'd trudged twenty hours carrying nearly our own body weight. All of us knackered, and dug-in Argy machine guns waiting to kill us. We'd never have got out if Colonel H Jones hadn't sacrificed himself.'

'I remember what he screamed, when he led that charge;' Steve said: '"*Come on, get your skirts off*".'

He expected a feminist protest from Helena, but all she said was, 'Joe, why did you go to the Falklands? A lot of us didn't think they were worth it. I'd say they weren't worth your life, or anybody else's.'

Chewing his food deliberately, and then drinking some more wine, Yatesy prepared his answer, eventually saying, 'Do you mean disobey orders? Have you any idea, Helena, how serious that is? I'd have been finished, and Carol too, if she stayed with me. You can't pick and choose in the army, you know. You go where you're sent, even if you might be killed. They don't want you to die, but they know some of you will have to. You know it too. But you still go.'

He paused again, and his eyes, which usually looked straight at people, seemed to be looking only into himself. 'When I was there I thought I might never come home to Carol. God knows, I've nothing against the Argies, or anybody in Northern Ireland. But I'm proud of what I've done.'

'You're right to be proud,' Steve answered, swigging a glass of wine as if it was water and wondering if Helena had ever had to go where she was sent, do what she was told. 'It's civil war in Northern Ireland, and the Falklands had been invaded. Nobody was going to sit down at a table over a meal and comfortably sort things out.'

'Steve, that's completely unfair,' Helena burst out. 'You're like a demagogic Marxist attacking the bourgeoisie, implying dinner tables are all I know about life. As a matter of fact I'd not sat down for so many meals for ages, till I met you.' Ignoring Yatesy's and Carol's alarmed glances at each other, she went on, 'Some people are too ready to fight. Mrs Thatcher talks about nothing but fighting, as if that Churchill speech about fighting on beaches and everywhere else spins in her brain night and day. Just to know she's alive she needs an enemy.'

'But Arthur Scargill wants a fight too,' Carol commented, speaking as she moved to an easy chair to be more comfortable. 'If he wins, where are we? We'd have no government. And why are people so violent - wives losing husbands, children losing fathers, in Northern Ireland? They could have everything we have.'

'For a long time Catholics in Northern Ireland couldn't have much the Protestants had,' Helena replied more calmly. 'We don't want to recognise it, but would these injustices have been attended to without a violent uprising? As for the Nationalist dimension, if Britain was occupied, as the Nationalists think Ireland is occupied, Mrs T would be the first over the barricades. She'd be like the woman in Delacroix's *Liberty Guiding the People*.'

Jesus, what's she referring to now, Steve thought. She thinks she's teaching a seminar. He was sure Carol and Yatesy didn't want this after their hard day. In fact Carol was closing her eyes, as if drifting into contented sleep.

He wondered why Helena couldn't recognise that for a lot of people opinions didn't matter, right or wrong. Some of his staff at the sports centre said things just to talk, make a noise, and join in. Encouraged by the probation service, he'd taken on a thirty-five-year- old ex-prisoner as a cleaner, help him make a new start and stay out of trouble. A hell of a good cleaner - spotless showers and bogs. But the daft bastard thought Norman Tebbitt was a member of the Labour Party, 'cos he's always causing bovver.' Steve didn't think his staff knew any facts about the money supply, or crime rates, or unmarried mothers - who did? They lived with kids to get to school, ailing parents to look after, bills to pay, cars to keep on the road, holidays to plan. Tabloid headlines, gossip, and rumour spiced things up, gave you something to chew on. But Helena couldn't allow you this kind of treat. She'd always read a *Guardian* article that told you you were wrong.

'I think Carol needs some rest,' Yatesy said, wanting to calm things down.

'Yes,' Carol said, sleepily. 'Half a glass of wine knocks me out. Bedtime for me. Thanks for such good food, Steve, and it's lovely to see you again, Helena. Do help yourself to some coffee. The cafetière's on the surface near the sink, and there's some cheese.'

She and Yatesy both stood up from the table, Yatesy putting his arm around her as they moved the staircase. It went up from the kitchen and had a door at the bottom. After Yatesy opened the door for Carol, Steve saw him hesitate, then follow Carol up the stairs.

Steve was sure Helena loved physical contact with him, but he didn't think he'd ever be able to put his arm around her protectively, as Yatesy had just done with Carol.

'I think we should go as soon as possible,' she now said. 'Forget the coffee. Give Carol and Joe some time to themselves.'

Standing up to clear the table Steve could almost see thoughts spinning in her mind, as if only her body was present in the room with him.

'There's an Emily Dickinson poem,' she said, still seated, and as if speaking to herself, 'about life as a loaded gun, about having the power only to kill. Was that what it was like as a soldier, kill or be killed, our inheritance of original sin?'

'I thought you didn't believe in religion. Anyway, I'm not in a poem.'

She looked up at him with a tense smile. 'I know you're not. You're warm and alive, thank God. Someone to hold on to.'

Getting up she moved into his open arms just as Yatesy re-appeared.

'Everything into the dishwasher, if we're clearing up,' he announced happily, glancing at them with a relieved smile. 'It's from a mate of mine in the electrical trade. My dad's always looked after his vans. I sweetheart him, and he sweethearts me, as they say. I've just given him a deal on six lovely panelled doors from a house we took down in Broadstairs.'

'"To sweetheart", what an unusual verb,' Helena said, as Steve released her.

'What you and Stevey are doing now, I hope,' Yatesy grinned. 'But not the same with me and my mate.'

'We're going to hit the road,' Steve said, as they'd loaded the dishwasher and tidied up. 'Give you and Carol some time to yourselves.'

'Right you are,' Yatesy replied, standing by his side, a couple of inches taller, and putting a heavy arm round his shoulders. 'Thanks again for the meal, Stevey.' Nodding towards Helena, he added 'We'll always enjoy seeing you both.'

'I haven't paid for the tiles,' she said.

'They're a gift,' Yatesy answered, 'to someone we hope will always be a friend, even when we don't see things the same way. If you like, let's say Stevey's cooking bought them for you.'

His big rough hands picked them up in the newspaper Carol had wrapped them in, and Steve saw it was a newspaper with the photograph of the O'Kanes and their priest. Yatesy saw it too, and looked at Steve as he gave the tiles to Helena and leaned forward to kiss her on the cheek, Helena meeting him halfway with a happy smile on her face.

In the car she immediately switched on the ten o'clock news.

Jesus, Steve thought, unsettled by the photograph. Miss the news for once, can't you? It won't have changed since we drove here.

Sure enough, it was again the latest on the miners, this time with a couple of Geordies saying how the country would soon be brought to its knees. At first Helena didn't even seem to be listening, but then she was all attention when Mick McGahey, leader of the Scottish miners, was interviewed and, in response to questions about the lack of ballot for the strike, announced, 'We won't be constitutionalised out of a strike!'

'There's a communist for you,' she said, turning to Steve and looking helpless. 'It's all we need.'

But feeling tensed up himself, he was already hitting the accelerator, making the car leap from forty to eighty-five on a very short, dark straight between Pett Bottom and Lower Hardres.

'Steve!' Helena yelled.

Holding the speed till they neared a bend, he pressed the brake pedal, seeing Helena brace her feet as she was thrust forward. Now he had her attention.

'What's this adolescent stuff?' she said, bewildered and upset, and switching the radio off. 'Why are you battling against me? You don't need to - ever. It doesn't matter if we see things differently. It's good for both of us.'

She was staying the night, and, as usual, he let her go upstairs first. Walking naked into the small main bedroom, which she'd lit by a dim table lamp, he knew she too would be naked under the duvet.

'Steady now, slowly,' she murmured as he knelt between her legs and began to kiss and caress her.

When he pushed gently into her, she wrapped her arms and legs around him, and he knew their bodies were now as together as two human bodies could ever be.

Briefly he thought of Simsy's body, in a box, deep in a hole in the ground. And the O'Kanes, somewhere.

VI

'Dead or alive, most likely dead, Portway's out of the loop,' Rick McKnight declared decisively. 'Nobody's any idea where that IRA team went after they left Sussex. We might as well put an ad on TV asking them to give us a call. Army family, public school, Sandhurst - Portway still couldn't handle himself.'

In the MI5 building towards noon Charles Furlow hardly listened to McKnight. Seated in his office behind his Edwardian mahogany desk, inherited from his father in the Foreign Office, his long fifty-four-year-old limbs, equally inherited, fitting comfortably into his father's chair, he was still pre-occupied by what he'd found on the desk first thing. So he simply registered again how McKnight's short powerful stature seemed to have been compacted into his exactingly measured suit. Whether McKnight's clothes were intended to conceal ruthlessness or advertise it remained for Furlow an open question. Similarly, he occasionally wondered if McKnight's meticulously razored sideburns were no more than a complement to the assertive baldness of the young man's head, or a threat of real menace.

'We'll have to let IRA matters look after themselves for a while,' he eventually responded. 'We're running short of people. We have Judith Rae and two other women planted at Greenham Common, and we need more infiltrators among the miners. We don't have a surplus of men with tattoos, big bellies and flat vowels.'

McKnight gestured a smile. Pushing thirty, and two years working under Furlow, he'd decided in his first week he'd be a loser if he responded to Furlow's pissy jokes.

Couldn't everybody see Furlow's lot were history; Portway the same? No idea about suppressing people like the miners, people who needed to be kept down.

'He hasn't a fuck left in him, so pay him off now,' he'd said last night in bed to Maddie.

'You're always fully loaded,' Maddie had responded.

Facing Furlow now, McKnight could still feel her small warm body lying half on top of him. She always met him at The True Compass in Southwark, appearing from nowhere. But he was sure she was safe. Had to be. No other woman gave him so much, did whatever he asked, loved his Canary Wharf apartment. With other women it was one night stands, if he was lucky, then forget it. Judith Rae, her red hair cut short like a boy's, hardly looked at him. She'd be up for Furlow's job if she weren't a woman.

'There's going to be no repeat of the miners' victories over Heath,' Furlow droned on, seeming to McKnight as if he was in a play. 'Establishment figures who plotted against Harold Wilson's Labour government still have their dander up, even in this building. They expect a Conservative prime-minister to field enough troops to finish off the miners, and any other bolshy unions. Finish off socialism.'

'Why not?' McKnight interjected.

'Already,' Furlow continued, 'we've phone taps on Scargill and McGahey personally, and on all the main union offices; a national police force in all but name. And now we must make absolutely certain there's mayhem at the miners' rallies, so the boys in blue can pitch in and save the nation from anarchy.'

'Get 'em by the balls, their hearts and minds will follow,' McKnight asserted, imagining himself as an American tough guy, a 'Dirty Harry'. 'Show them who's in control. Make a profit or else! That three-day week under Heath was Third World. I was at university. No hot water, heating; nothing you could do when it was dark' (except shag, he remembered).

'The miners believe the work they have is the only real work there'll ever be for them,' Furlow replied.

'They believe anything that bastard Scargill tells them. One of them's already got himself killed on a picket-line. We could do with more results like that, and we'll get them at Orgreave.'

'What! What are you saying?' Suddenly Furlow found some passion. 'Are you confirming what I'm hearing - that there are plans for a violent battle with the miners up at that coking plant in Yorkshire in June? Is this what Minter has in mind?'

'You tell me,' McKnight responded, knowing Furlow couldn't, because he wasn't in on Vigilance, the special task force set up by new MI5 big wheel, David Minter, who'd been brought back from America, where he'd been hooked up with the CIA for over a dozen years. For McKnight Minter and Vigilance were the future, especially when it came to anticipating and aborting anything broadly defined as civil disobedience.

'I need to make a move,' he now declared, determined to leave Furlow's office while he thought he was ahead. 'Get on Portway's trail.'

'I suppose so,' Furlow replied resignedly.'

Making sure the door was closed after McKnight had left, Furlow sat in silence for a few minutes. Then he took from a drawer the torn half of an A4 photograph waiting on his desk when he arrived first thing this morning. It had been inside what jokes referred to as a 'plain brown envelope', unnervingly unsealed. How it got there he'd no idea. It showed Guy Portway in his captain's uniform in front of a Saracen, with Paul and James O'Kane in handcuffs on his right slumped against the Saracen; both of them badly beaten up, and Paul O'Kane with a shoulder wound visibly bleeding.

Furlow knew when the photograph must have been taken: South Tyrone, March 1981, after the ambush of the IRA unit to capture the O'Kanes had gone scandalously wrong, and he'd had to invent a cover story about heroism against the odds to placate the media and the grieving families of the three British soldiers who'd been killed. He hadn't personally delivered the cover story to the media, but his prints as the author were all over it. Obviously this photograph of Portway and the O'Kanes was a threat to unravel it and blow it apart.

But a threat from where? Who'd taken the photograph? How was it delivered onto his desk this morning, at a time when the IRA was starting to probe the O'Kanes' disappearance, and there were pictures in the papers and on TV showing them to be two innocent Catholic young men?

Who knows if the IRA has a presence in this building, Furlow asked himself, not sure he wanted to take the question further, since it might expose twenty years of his own covert activity in the affairs of Northern Ireland.

And what about the missing half of the torn photograph? Who or what, if anything, was on that?

Better take this home, he thought, sliding the photograph back into the envelope, sealing it, and slipping it into his briefcase. No point in destroying it, because somebody knows I have it, and there must be other copies, even in desks close to mine. Perhaps leave it with Beatrice to be opened if something untoward happens. With her prominence in the media, nobody better than his daughter Beatrice to exploit such a thing, even if she might well exploit it as much for her own benefit as his.

'Lunch time already Charles?'

It was Minter's mid-Atlantic voice from further along the corridor, catching Furlow locking his office door, even as he wondered why he bothered to do so.

Turning, Furlow was aware again of Minter's habitually ambiguous smile. He'd had worn it on his first day, a month ago, making his opaque announcement that, 'We need new synergies, an American perspective, pre-emptiveness.'

'Some fresh air,' Furlow responded, nodding in Minter's direction, and continuing on his way out. He'd never crossed the

Atlantic and was convinced American perspectives were no more than American paranoia, worth about as much as the Kentucky Fried chicken bones and boxes he kicked towards a spewing waste bin, as he waited for his taxi.

'Covent Garden,' he commanded the driver.

He was looking forward to the relief of having lunch with his friend Peter Edwards, Peter's daughter Helena, and a man she'd met in her new job at Canterbury University. He and Peter had been close friends since they were both at Oxford, where Peter had stayed more or less all his life, and they often met for lunch whenever Peter was in London, as he was today to examine a Ph.D.

As students, Furlow remembered, they'd kept pace with each other towards their Firsts in History, and were still inclined to use the other as a yardstick. Their daughters, Helena and Beatrice, had been at boarding-school together and had stayed at each other's houses in their early teens, after which they'd drifted apart. Furlow still remembered his own son James, already fat and double-chinned at twenty-five, and on his way to becoming a barrister, paying special attention to Helena on one of these visits.

'She has the makings of a suitable wife, when she grows up,' James had announced around the breakfast table after Helena had returned home.

'Not for you,' Beatrice told him immediately.

Furlow hadn't seen Helena for some time, but kissing her cheek and shaking Steve Wilson's hand in the restaurant, he straight away had a sense of what Beatrice had meant a dozen or so years ago with regard to James. Even in the army after university Furlow had never been so close to such an obviously fit young man, while Helena, judging by the glowing health leaping out of her trim body, seemed modelled to match him. Poor Peter, stooping between them, grey of complexion, and always troubled by asthma, hardly looked to belong to the same species. I must keep up my weekend swimming, Furlow thought, reminded, in the presence of these two apparent athletes, of his recent inconclusive check-up with his doctor, and his doctor's impenetrable observation that there was 'nothing to worry about for a man of your age.'

'We're thinking of Dover sole, Charles, to celebrate Kent,' Peter announced, 'and I've ordered a Chablis. I don't know about you, but all the rest of us have the afternoon off. Helena and Steve are going to the Barbican this evening to see *Macbeth*. I'm looking forward to a snooze on the train back to Oxford.'

'Lucky you, Peter,' Furlow responded, 'though, as it happens, I've not much on my desk. I might well go home myself.'

The waiter hovered. He offered to take Furlow's briefcase, but Furlow gestured he would keep it by his feet.

'We never ask what Charles does for a living,' Peter smiled to Steve. 'As you can see, whatever it is it's kept him in better condition than Oxford has kept me.'

'How's Beatrice nowadays,' Helena asked. 'I haven't seen her for years, though I know she's always in the papers and on the telly.'

'Not the kind of things you read and watch, I'm sure,' Furlow said.

Helena shook her head, 'Not regularly. That show of hers, *In Their Shoes*, women celebrities in their bedrooms or dressing rooms gossiping about other celebrities, while they display how many shoes they've got, and say when they bought them and why - no, that's not for me.'

'My mother and sister are really into that show,' Steve Wilson asserted. 'They're interested in women's stuff, shoes and things. My sister says it's something you can just flop down to after a hard shift. She's a senior nurse,' he added, 'on the go all day.'

'My wife and other daughter, who's a GP, older than Beatrice, like it too,' Furlow responded, noticing the questioning look Helena gave Steve. 'But my son, who's never really got on with

Beatrice, bans it from his house. His wife and daughters have to come to our house to watch videos of the programme in secret.'

As they ate their fish, Furlow noticed how delicately, for a big man, Steve Wilson cut into it, matching the care with which he tasted the Chablis. Helena, by contrast, seemed to eat and drink without much consciousness of what she was putting into her mouth.

'Before he got the job running the sports centre at Canterbury, Steve was in the army,' Peter said. 'Northern Ireland and the Falklands. Charles started in the army,' he added for Steve's benefit. 'Myself, I didn't even do National Service - asthma.'

'See any action?' Steve asked Furlow.

'Too much in Kenya, in the Fifties, during our new Elizabethan Age,' Furlow responded. Relishing the wine, he went on, 'How could it not be the same as any other age, requiring young men to die *pro patria*? Trapped in one more of history's ironies we were there to exterminate the Mau Mau. Some of them had fought under the British flag against Hitler.'

'*History is a nightmare from which I am trying to awake,*' Helena contributed. Receiving blank looks, she apologised, 'Sorry, I'm quoting again.'

'I was commanding conscripts,' Furlow continued, 'working class chaps like the miners; salt of the earth, you might say, except when some of them got their hands on native women.'

'Actually, I'm trying to get Steve to see things from the miners' point of view,' Helena responded.

'Nothing wrong with that,' Peter said.

'We certainly need to arrange these pit closures with a bit more imagination,' Furlow agreed, by way of an aside. 'The way things are going we might never need the miners' kind of physical strength ever again. Nobody's giving any thought as to how these men will spend their days when their jobs are gone. It's as if we're 'accepting we'll only ever need a few of them, and that will be to keep the rest of them down.'

'If that happens, there'll be more riots like Brixton and Toxteth,' Helena declared. 'People won't accept a lifetime of no hope.'

'Do you see things from the miners' point of view, Steve?' Furlow asked.

'Sometimes. My brother-in-law's a miner.'

'In any event, you'll know what I'm saying about Kenya. All the authority and discipline in the world won't control what some men get up to in a war.'

'I've experience of that,' Steve agreed. 'Even when they're back here, some of them still lose it. There's the soldier who's killed the girl in Canterbury because she was stringing him along. She lived a couple of streets away from me.' To Furlow in particular he said, '"The Carmen Killing" your daughter calls it, in her "Beatrice" column.'

'Where do you read the "Beatrice" column?' Helena exclaimed, amazed.

'One of the women on the reception desk at the sports centre brought in her Sunday tabloid.'

'You need to be careful when you say the girl was stringing the soldier along,' Helen said firmly. 'It might imply she was asking for whatever happened to her. She may have behaved foolishly, but she wasn't asking to be killed.'

Steve raising his hands before his chest as if in surrender, she turned to explain to her father.

'The young woman, nineteen, was called Vicky Jordan. She had an affair with a soldier, stationed in Canterbury, while her partner, a would-be pop singer, was entertaining on a cruise ship. When the partner went for another tour on the ship, the soldier appeared at her flat again, but neighbours heard Vicky Jordan turning him down. They also heard a violent quarrel, in which the soldier hit her and broke her neck. Appalling!'

'Indeed,' her father said.

'"Carmen Killing" was Beatrice's invention,' Furlow confirmed, after there had been a moment's silence. 'If you want to know its origin, it actually jumped into her head while she, my wife and I were seeing *Carmen* a few weeks ago, just across the way from here.'

'Beatrice's husband is Simon Gallagher, the millionaire pop music producer,' Helena explained to her father.

'Useful,' Peter commented, as he emptied what was left of the Chablis into Steve's glass, no-one else wanting more wine.

'Yes,' Furlow agreed. 'Simon's useful, but he very rarely takes part in the delights he arranges for the rest of the family.'

'Reclusive?' Helena asked.

'He seems to prefer living with all the technology of his recording studio, and when he's at home he's often in the fully equipped gym in the basement of their house, which is in Connaught Square.' Looking at Steve, Furlow added, 'But I rather see him as ascetic rather than athletic.'

No-one taking this point up, Furlow continued, 'As for Beatrice, you're never sure where her mind is, or what level it's working on. When she blurted out "Carmen Killing" and declared immediately she now had an angle for her weekend commentary on the soldier who'd killed the girl in Canterbury, I was completely exasperated, because she seemed to be taking no interest in the opera itself, the music and so on. I said to her, "Bizet didn't write this opera just to give you a headline." But all she replied was, "Do you think he'd mind?"'

'I hear that Wes's, her husband's famous recording-studio used to be a Wesleyan Methodist chapel,' Helena said.

'I think John Wesley would mind,' Furlow joked.

Steve had now finished off the Chablis, Furlow noticing again the attention he continued to give it. Immediately they moved straight on to the coffee with some chocolates, and soon it was time for the bill, which Furlow and Peter paid with their credit cards.

'It's been a pleasure to meet you,' he said to Steve, as they all said their good-byes on the pavement outside the restaurant, Steve having handed him his briefcase when they left their table. He kissed Helena, shook hands with Peter, and then, more firmly, with Steve. 'Enjoy the *Macbeth*,' he said. 'If enjoy is the right word for that play.'

He meant it about the pleasure, especially after the morning he'd had with the photograph weighing on his mind. All through lunch he'd been refreshed by the presence of Helena and Steve, warming to his sense of their young promise. On his train to Sevenoaks, looking forward to the remaining daffodils greeting him in his garden, and the familiar comforts of his Lutyens-style house, he reflected that Peter could no more have imagined Helena being in a relationship with someone like Steve than he could have imagined Beatrice marrying Simon.

Peter and he had married girls from their own social class, his wife Marjorie being, to his eyes, the pick of Kenya's Rift Valley and eager for a new life in England. Perhaps, he mused, Beatrice was the newest life they'd ever actually had - refusing to go to university, working for a pop music newspaper, and bringing home a penniless, Irish, self-taught recording engineer who, almost over-night, had become a multi-millionaire from the proceeds of several international best-selling albums, all recorded in studios he rented (with Beatrice's money) pre-Wes's.

'Don't let this out,' Beatrice said to him, as Wes's became pre-eminent. 'All the guitar solos for the groups Simon produces are played by a tiny man from West Hartlepool called Shane Webb, who's had a spinal injury from birth. It doesn't matter what the group's called, or who its lead guitarist is supposed to be. Everything's deception in the recording studio.'

Simon, Furlow soon understood, dealt in illusions, and this evening, he reflected, Helena and Steve would be indulging in another kind of illusion, until they left the theatre to come out into the real. Doubtless they would think about the connections between the real and the play they'd just seen, but, between the two, they'd probably be confident they knew more or less where they were. *Macbeth*, after all, was an acknowledged illusion to which you willingly submitted for a limited time. Simon's illusions, by contrast, were unacknowledged. Only a few people knew who was really playing the guitar solos.

Simon's world, Furlow recognised, was like the covert world, though obviously less menacing. The covert world touched people without their cognisance, so that even a Helena and a Steve, in all their uprightness, might not be able to know the ground they stood on. At Orgreave, where Minter would be staging a spectacular confrontation, Furlow was certain the miners wouldn't know this ground.

In fact, he had to concede, he was losing contact with it himself, despite a lifetime's conscious involvement in the covert. There was the torn photograph found on his desk this morning, but there was also the passing of life itself, separating you from yourself. Furlow knew that talking about Kenya during lunch was merely reciting lines he'd delivered at countless dinner parties, lines no longer meaningful to him, as if the experience behind them belonged to someone else. Everything, it seemed, might become illusion - except death, which might be imminently threatened for someone by a missive from the covert world concealed in his briefcase.

VII

Steve couldn't get over *Macbeth*, the first live play he'd seen since an unwatchable school production of *Julius Caesar*, with the cast drawn from both boys' and girls' grammar schools.

At the Barbican he discovered Shakespeare knew all about being in a savage battle and chopping into another man, like the bayonet charges on the Falklands, when the Paras were at Mount Longdon and Wireless Ridge above Stanley; life meeting death all around you, no sense to anything, except trying to stay alive yourself. Shakespeare knew too about women hanging out with soldiers, tempting you like the witches, who, sometimes in this production, were like ordinary women; maybe tempting you to your death; plenty of that in Northern Ireland.

He'd never seen anything like the staging, which was mostly platforms on scaffolding. At one exit Macbeth, a big man, thrilled Steve by leaping up from one platform to the next, as if trying to catch up with his own life. Yes, Macbeth did terrible things, but first of all he'd had to do terrible things for the king, when everybody praised him; just like Mrs Thatcher and the government praising the soldiers coming back from the Falklands, no questions asked about what the soldiers had had to do. Steve couldn't settle for Macbeth being a villain, a monster. Macbeth understood too much, saw what others didn't want to look at. Watching the play, Steve suddenly remembered Simsy: 'Me and you, we've been there. We know what it's all about; what has to be done.'

'*Vaulting ambition,*' Helena quoted, when he referred to the actor's leap.

It was six o'clock on a Saturday evening in May. They were in Steve's lounge, Steve in a bathrobe ready to take a shower.

Helen had driven over to his place, and later they were going to a housewarming before spending the night at Steve's.

'*Vaulting ambition*,' Steve quoted back. 'I like that. A bit like me, I suppose, when I left school to sign on for United. After they'd seen me in the last trial, they told me to get changed and wait in a room. They sent a secretary, who led me into her office to sign the forms. I couldn't turn it down. It seemed like such a big chance to become somebody.'

'I'm sure she wasn't a witch.'

'She was very good-looking, about ten years older than me at the time, about your age now.'

'I wonder if you would have gone her into her office if she hadn't been good-looking. Maybe United sent her to seduce you into signing the forms.'

He shrugged, then said, 'Macbeth and me - we both failed.'

'It must have been a huge blow for you,' Helena responded, softly touching his shoulder, and moving her body into his as he put his arm around her waist.

'Better believe it. It was the first time I was told I wasn't good enough for something I really wanted to do. I'd never had a door slammed in my face before.'

'But I'm told all the university football fanatics still think you should have become a professional.'

'What do they know? Just because I play a few five-a-side games in the sports centre. They've no idea how good you have to be to make it professionally.' Turning to face her with his hands on her shoulders, he insisted, 'Let's get this straight and then finish with it. I left school after O levels, because I had the chance of playing for one of the greatest football clubs in the world. But after three years United dumped me.'

She moved close to him again, putting her arms around his neck. 'Knowing you,' she said, 'I bet there was more to it than that.

Anyway, not to succeed at something at such a young age - don't let it wound your whole life.'

In the shower to get ready for the party, Steve's United days came back to him, especially Alex Graham, killed in a drunken car crash in Glasgow on his brother's stag night the summer Steve joined the army.

United had him in digs with Alex, who, with his curly, shoulder-length blond hair and slight build, looked to Steve anything but a footballer. But give him a ball, and anybody could see he was extra special; a very fast, nearly unstoppable left-sided front player, with a big future.

And a big appetite for sex. No problem for him fixing up two nurses after morning training - Steve's first time, when he was seventeen.

'You footballers,' he remembered his nurse sighing, both of them exhausted, as they finally lay together in her bed at the nurses' hostel. 'You're so firm and fit and clean from the showers. I couldn't wait to get into bed with you. You should see some of the old dying bodies I see all day. Sometimes you can hardly tell whether they're men or women, no matter where you look.'

Nearing the end of his three-year contract, when he was nearly nineteen, Steve felt he'd made steady progress in the reserve teams, though there were centre-backs in front of him, one of them an England international. He was still mates with Alex, who'd had games with the first team. At any level football came easily to Alex, but Steve was beginning to understand it needed total effort with him. Playing against Alex your whole game could fall apart. Stay touch-tight, he still turned and danced round you. Back off to give yourself distance and time, a spectator on the terraces had as much chance of stopping him.

Lightning-quick.

At a practice game in late April of that third year he skinned Steve twice in the first fifteen minutes. Then, four inches shorter than Steve, he moved ahead of him at a corner and headed a goal. So when he came again down the left Steve went at him with both feet off the ground like a missile (he could still see himself), sliding at a ball that had gone when he arrived and hooking Alex viciously up in the air.

Immediately there was a barging gaggle of players, some of them ready with their fists.

In the shower, looking back on it, Steve knew he'd gone into that tackle to destroy Alex. He wondered about the violence in himself and maybe in all men. He couldn't imagine Helena being violent, or Carol, though he knew his sister wouldn't be bossed around. 'You'll get nowhere working in the National Health Service, if you don't stand up for yourself,' she'd told him.

Then he was back at that practice game, hearing Stan Cummings, the Assistant Manager, bellow at the barging scrum of players, 'Get apart. Stop swinging and kicking at one another. You all play for the same fucking club!'

I'd become a Cummings, when I pulled Yatesy and the others off the O'Kanes, Steve thought, generously spreading shower gel over himself. But he knew he'd never forget Cummings' next words to him, because they started to change his life.

'Stevey, my office when you're dressed,' Cummings said.

Sitting and facing Cummings across a battered desk in Cummings' shed of an office on the training ground, he learned the news.

'I'm sorry, Stevey, but we're letting you go. We won't be giving you another contract after this summer.'

He remembered looking at Cummings' receding grey hair, the arcs of skin at each side of a thin central strip. Cummings had been a very good first division goalie.

'What have I done wrong? Was it that tackle?'

'Fuck the tackle. Alex was asking for it, and it'll teach him to get out of the way. There'll be plenty more where that came from.'

'What then?'

'C'mon, Stevey. You're a bright lad. What is it, eight O levels, same as my daughter? You must've reckoned up. Look who else we've got. And I'm not saying you're finished. In fact I've found another club for you. Have a good pre-season with them, you could go straight into their first team.'

Then he named Bilston Rovers, a second division club.

'Their manager could be United's next manager. And you know what; I think you could be a manager one day. I could be wrong, but I'm not sure you're going to make it as a player in the first division.'

Cummings, in his middle fifties, was a kind man, and Steve remembered that after he'd said this he stood up and went to open a drawer of a metal filing cabinet. He must have delivered similar verdicts to a few hundred young hopefuls, and, hearing their world collapse, some of them, no matter how tough on the playing pitch, would have had tears in their eyes. Better, Cummings must have thought, to turn away for a few moments, so as not to see tears and not to add to any sense of humiliation.

But in the shower Steve, looking back on himself at nearly nineteen in Cummings' office, also recalled himself as a seven year old, standing alone in the playground of his primary school, after an older boy had punched him hard in the stomach. As that seven year old, he was vowing to himself, 'Nobody will ever see me cry.' So, devastated as he was by Cummings' news, there were no tears for Cummings to turn away from.

'No matter how hard you train, you'll never stay with the Alexes of this world,' Cummings continued, again sitting himself down to face Steve across the desk; 'But you're a very good leader, and you can read a game. I've seen how the other lads listen to you, and do what you tell 'em. You learn your trade from the bottom up, earn your coaching badges, and I'll put money on you running a big club before you're my age. Remember, a lot of the best managers have not been great players. Off a football field Alex can just about manage himself into a girl's knickers.'

But when his contract ended in the summer, and just after he turned nineteen, Steve remembered how, without an appointment, he walked into the army recruiting office in Atherstone and signed on for what was called an 'Open Engagement', a contract without any time limit. He did it just as single-mindedly as when he signed on for United; except this time, because he didn't tell anybody till it was done, and because he wasn't at school any longer, there was hardly any publicity in his local paper, and no row with disappointed teachers. His life would be on his terms and nobody else's.

VIII

The housewarming was at Mike and Catherine Connery's. Mike was a colleague of Helena's in the English Department, but he also chaired the university Sports and Recreation Committee, which was responsible for the sports centre. He'd been on the panel appointing Steve as an assistant and had then made sure Steve got the directorship.

'We needed a tough bastard to get this new show on the road,' Steve remembered Mike saying to him before the last appointment, 'and my money's on you. You've disappointed nobody as an assistant. You've lived up to everything your commanding officer said about you in his reference. I'd no idea how self-motivated you had to be to become a corporal in the short time you did it.'

Mike had also been a running partner for Steve ever since Steve arrived at the university, and he still occasionally ran with Steve and Helena. He was nearly ten years older than Steve, about his height but not as heavy and solid, so whenever their runs together speeded up, say the last half mile back to the sports centre, he always beat Steve, causing Steve to wonder if Mike was another Alex Graham, another a bloke doing easily what he could only do hard. Helena was sure Mike would soon become a Professor, and to Steve he always seemed comfortable in his own skin, taking open pleasure in his home life with his wife Catherine and four children. Catherine, who worked occasionally as a supply teacher, sang in several local choirs, so when Steve visited their house there were usually music scores opened on surfaces and music stands he was careful not to knock over. He liked the whole family and, using DIY skills learned from Gordon, his brother, had helped them get their new house ready.

The house was on a recent 'executive' housing estate in the Rough Common area in the North of Canterbury, not far from Steve's own house. It meant Helena and Steve could walk to the party, which was well under way when they arrived. Greeted warmly with their bottles by Catherine, they made their way into a lounge that went the full length of one side of the house and was extended at the back into an impressive conservatory. Amid the drinking and talking, a music system played background jazz.

Mike having supplied them with them with drinks, Steve checked the other guests warily. There were some people he recognised, regular users of the sports centre, but one of these he knew immediately he would avoid. This was Jim Kearney, a Professor of Sociology and member of the local Labour Party, who'd led a campaign against all the new sports centre charges, arguing they violated the university's obligation to provide for the well-being of the campus community, whose labour already earned university recreational facilities. While he was still an assistant at the sports centre, Steve had stood at the back of a meeting packing the university's biggest lecture hall, listening to Kearney attack the 'Thatcherisation, the marketisation, of every aspect of life'.

But then worse had followed from Kearney. Born in Dublin but brought up in London, where he'd gone to the LSE, he'd stirred things up about the O'Kanes as soon as their photos were all over the media. Posters nailed to campus trees shouted, WHAT'S HAPPENED TO THE O'KANES?, as they invited everyone to another meeting chaired by Kearney, though this time there were only about thirty people, including Helena and her friend, Jan Woodhouse, the politics lecturer Helena had been to Greenham Common with.

'How do people involved in such a dirty business as the O'Kanes' sleep at night?' Helena had murmured to Steve, snuggling into his arms in his bed at the end of the day of that meeting.

In fact both she and Jan detested Kearney, even though he was a fellow Labour member. They thought his attitude to women was entirely sexual.

'As he walks towards you, you can see him taking your clothes off,' Helena had protested to Steve. 'Every year he beds a final year woman student, knowing she'll soon leave, as if it's a natural perk of his job.'

Slightly stooped with long greying curly hair and a straggling moustache, Kearney, about fifty, was married to a younger wife who was the heiress of a London Estate Agency fortune. There were two very young daughters, but eighteen months ago Kearney's wife had dramatically taken the children and left him for a man closer to her own age. Now, at the party, Kearney was apparently on his own and already tanked up. When Steve looked at him, his face was venomous. Steve knew he would never forget that on his first day as director, Kearney had called him a 'fascist', when he'd made Kearney pay for a game of squash.

Turning to the rest of the gathering, Steve saw that Helena had immediately joined her friend Jan. From Jan Steve always sensed political hostility, which he tended to think was also hostility to his relationship with Helena. Jan knew he thought Mrs Thatcher was right: uneconomic pits should close. He hoped this night out wouldn't be ruined by hearing her say again, 'All economics are political.'

He was impressed though that she'd been on TV, on *Newsnight*, and been interviewed on radio, on *The World at One*, always defending the miners and claiming Mrs Thatcher secretly intended to wipe out the entire coal industry. Till he met Jan, the only people he'd come across who'd been on telly were star footballers at United and high ranking army officers. During her last interview on *Newsnight*, Jan had announced she was organising accommodation in the Canterbury area for miners' kids who would be on their way to across the Channel for a holiday provided by French unions.

As Steve got together with Helena and Jan, Max Freedman, who taught Economics, came across to them. He was short but powerfully built, with dark stubble already erupting on his newly shaved face, and chest hairs thrusting irrepressibly through his open-necked shirt. He hung on to the lecturers' five-a-side crowd, playing with more enthusiasm than skill.

'If you even roll a ball to him,' Steve had told Helena, 'he hops round it from foot to foot as if it's a live grenade. He just can't relate to it.'

Max was married to Rebecca Rabinowitz, an American who was finishing a PhD in Politics and being supervised by one of Jan's male colleagues. She was, according to Jan, 'a rabid Republican.'

'Nice modern house this,' Max said. 'Trouble-free, I imagine. Now me, I can't seem to live without a hole in the roof and dodgy plumbing. What a fantasy of mine our country cottage in Wickhambreaux was. That's why Rebecca's been to visit her parents in New Jersey - so she can flush a toilet.' Turning to Jan, who wasn't smiling, he added, ' I'm sorry, Jan. There's no chance of us putting up your evacuees, even if Rebecca would agree.'

'Can't the plumbing be fixed?' Steve asked. 'There's nothing to the way a toilet system works.'

'Don't start to describe it now, Steve,' Helena said.

'But it's not a mystery,' he insisted; then, sensing three faces looking at him blankly, he stopped. Sod it, he thought, they don't want to know. It's like when you try to tell them about plugs and points and carburettors, when their cars won't start. They just glaze over.

Suddenly affection for his brother swept through him. He could see Gordon's garage with the tools neatly arranged along its walls and the cans of oil and paint on its shelves. Gordon's Rover 2000 never went more than ten miles beyond any service it needed, Gordon doing most of it himself. He remembered when he was last in Atherstone and helped Gordon fix the brakes on the Rover; how vulnerable the back of Gordon's neck looked as he knelt down to slide in the new disc-pads. After being in the army you could never forget how easily a man could be killed. In the Falklands they'd walked behind kneeling Argies, touching the backs of their necks with the muzzles of automatic weapons, scaring them shitless, making themselves feel safe. 'Always brush their balls,' an experienced Para told him on his first tour of Northern Ireland, when they were searching men who had been made to face a wall, spread-eagled. 'It keeps 'em on edge.'

'I have to assume there'll be enough accommodation for the miners' children,' Jan was insisting to Max. 'Helena's putting two girls up on camp beds in her lounge.'

Drawing powerfully on her cigarette, till Steve thought he heard it whistle, Jan seemed to him to be very wound up. Suddenly he remembered Helena telling him Jan had just been turned down for promotion to a Professorship, though her teaching and research were highly rated. There were rumours the rejection was because of her very public presence at Greenham Common and support for the miners. But Helena had also told Steve that Jan was one of many women academics nationally whose careers were not being advanced nearly as quickly as men's. So Jan's articles in newspapers and appearances on TV had been judged irrelevant to her promotion, though normally, Helena told Steve, 'If a male lecturer so much as has a coffee in a TV studio, the university PR machine makes sure the whole world knows about it. Payback time for the big chief's knighthood,' she added, referring to Canterbury University's Vice Chancellor. 'He's buddies with half the cabinet from his student days.'

'You should be happy with what you're doing for the miners,' Max was now saying consolingly to Jan. 'That piece you did in *The*

Guardian the other day, making their case, was as good as it gets, even if I don't entirely agree with it.'

But now his wife, Rebecca, joined them, hearing what he'd just said.

'It still beats me why this guy Scargill has so much support,' she interjected. 'What does he offer us women? And is it seriously being argued no uneconomic mines should ever be closed down? No wonder Britain's been a basket case for over a decade.'

'Oh yeah,' said Jan, ignoring the comment about women. 'It's so easy for the well paid to write off the jobs of the poorly paid. Thatcher made sure she married a fortune before she declared nobody owed anybody a living.'

'What's wrong with the deal the miners are being offered?' Rebecca challenged. 'Nobody's being fired, and there's good money for anybody who quits voluntarily.'

'Bribery!' Jan retorted. 'What happens if they take the money, spend it and then find they have no jobs?'

'Can't they move, go where the work is, retrain, go back to school?' Rebecca countered. 'What is it with people over here? Forget your politics. All your attitudes are so conservative. People in the States can always feel themselves moving ahead, but you're all so trapped in the past. Look at Northern Ireland. Have you seen the actual streets they're fighting over? Who'd want to live in them?'

'*God Bless America*,' Jan exclaimed, 'except Americans forget the words are supposed to be a prayer and not a command.' Her voice becoming shrill, she went on, 'Don't you all see, it's politics and not economics? Destroy the trade-unions, obliterate ideological choice, fix the world so there's only capitalism or capitalism, entirely Americanised. Take this job at this price, or get lost. Some democracy. As if democracy weren't always bought and sold in America.'

'I suppose you prefer Scargill's entirely Eastern European communism, plus miners' rallies that are more like Nuremberg rallies,' Rebecca declared. 'I remind you there's been no democratic ballot to legitimise this strike.' Looking away from Jan's strained white face, she exclaimed to Helena, 'As for your Labour Party, somebody tell me what alternative it's offering. All it gives you is the chance to feel moral, about the miners and all sorts of other issues, even about America. The anti-Americanism over here drives me crazy. Capitalism guarantees freedom. We were at your side in two world wars.'

'Look, Rebecca, I don't want to debate all this now,' Helena responded. 'I'm depressed enough about politics. Labour's hopeless, and Mrs Thatcher's replaced God in much of Britain.' Seeing Steve looking bored, she still persisted, 'We just can't tell thousands of families their way of life's a right-off, start again. Members of the cabinet have hardly ever changed their way of life. They've always lived in a perpetual senior common room. They only want change for everybody else.'

'Let's leave all this,' Max said.

'This wine's doing nothing for me,' Steve announced. Putting a hand over his wine-glass, as Mike appeared with a bottle of white and a bottle of red, he said, 'I need a beer.' Under his breath he muttered, 'I might need ten beers, so I know I'm having a good time! Call this a bleeding party!'

He moved into the garden end of the conservatory, where there were cans of beer and bowls of crisps and nuts. Some people were standing on the patio, though it wasn't all that warm. Cracking open a can and relishing the hoppy taste of the Kent Shepherd Neame bitter, he noticed Helena had begun talking to the Polish academic who was at Canterbury University on some sort of exchange scheme.

From Scargill's communist world, he thought; so bad everybody's having to give her stuff to take back, toothpaste and

Tampax, for fuck's sake. Wasn't Rebecca right about taking your chances and improving yourself? That's what his brother Gordon had done with an Open University degree, and so had Linda, his sister, passing all her nursing exams till she was earning as much as her husband and able to support the family while he was striking with the Lancashire miners.

As he opened a second can, he noticed Jim Kearney had moved to a position where he could assess Helena side on and gloat over the outlines of her breasts.

Suddenly, he felt jealousy hitting him like a blow in the chest. He wanted to block Kearney's view of Helena, wanted everybody at the party to know Helena was *his*, and, tonight, would be in *his* bed, nobody else's.

In his bed, he gave her everything she wanted.

He remembered once, when he came first, body and brain completely blown from him, she had had an even bigger orgasm and then, after lying quietly by his side for several minutes, had begun to sing softly in an American accent, '*Anythin you can do, I can do bedder.*'

In the sack, together, they were great.

Catherine was at his side, bringing him back into the party. 'You should be getting something to eat,' she said, her voice full and rich from all the singing she did.

'I'm sure it'll be good,' he replied.

'Wait till you see the pear tart, or *tarte aux poires Provencale*. When it comes out of the oven, it makes you happy just to look at it. It's flavoured with Kirsch, and there's cream in it, but it won't put weight on your body.' Looking him up and down, she added 'I know you don't do desserts. Our youngest calls them "deserves", and who deserves more from us than you?'

He smiled happily at Catherine who always relaxed him.

'I don't go in for all this fitness malarkey,' she'd told him when he first met her, and as if to justify a figure that showed she'd had children; 'though you should try singing Beethoven's *Missa Solemnis* or Britten's *War Requiem*.'

'Not Steve's bag,' Mike had declared.

From Helena Steve had learned Mike and Catherine were childhood sweethearts, like Yatesy and Carol.

Catherine had carried on the cookery lessons where Steve's sister-in-law had left off. Knowing he followed recipes as strictly as he read maps in the army, Catherine suggested extra spices, and told him to save the water from the cooked vegetables for making the sauce. From her he learned about de-glazing a pan. But he knew she was a challenge to Helena and other women academics.

'She asked me if I read Elizabeth David,' Helena said to him a few weeks ago; 'as if that's as important as great literature. She sings, sews, cooks, brings up the children - all the traditional domestic stuff. There's a whole side of life Mike needn't bother about. He can just move on with his career, something other colleagues with less conventional arrangements can't do.'

'But her singing takes a lot of time,' Steve replied. 'She goes to different choir practices three nights a week. I've been there when Mike's been putting the kids to bed and reading to them. He does his share.'

Once, when Mike and he were running together, Mike told him, 'Catherine's the creative force in our relationship: food, clothes, music; all the colours for the house; designs for the garden. Sometimes I think I'm just an academic hack - sterile, living off other people's imagination. I do all this reading, writing, thinking (if you can call it that); ask all sorts of questions - and there she is, the centre of what my life's really about.'

Suddenly Steve was brought back to the present by a disturbance at the front end of the lounge. He saw a man down on the floor with blood dripping from his nose. Jim Kearney was standing over him shouting, 'Get back to my bitch of a wife, and don't come in here and tell me how to look after my kids.'

Talking to Kearney, Mike was trying to calm things down.

'Jim, let him up.'

Kearney backed off, but then, in a frenzy, rushed to put his boot into the man on the floor. He was only prevented because Steve had moved across the room to shoulder-charge and flatten him. Kearney fell amid four people who immediately moved away.

Bending over Kearney, Steve had his right fist drawn back and clenched. Raising his left arm towards Steve, the palm open and fingers stretched apart. Kearney said, 'OK. Let it be.'

Steve stood back, giving him space to get up, but tensed and ready, his fist now clenched at his side.

Mike helped Kearney up.

'Come on, Jim,' he said. 'I think it would be best for everybody if you went home. Do it for your kids' sake, if for nobody else's.'

'You're right,' Kearney said. 'That's enough. I'm sorry this had to happen at your party, Mike.'

Signalling for Steve to move away, Mike steered Kearney to the door leading to the hall, but as they reached it Kearney turned back contemptuously at Steve.

'You jock ignoramus! I'll see to it you're fired! I'll have you done for assault!'

Then he left the room.

After some minutes the front door closed, and Mike came back. He joined Catherine, who was now attending to the man Kearney had slapped. He wasn't badly injured. Nobody knew him, and now that he was safe he was mainly red with embarrassment.

'I'm all right,' he said. 'I'll just leave. I've a spare pair of glasses in the car. That guy's a madman, dangerous. You see what Denise has had to put up with all these years. I had to come and get him. He's supposed to be looking after the girls this weekend. He left them alone in his house. They're seven and nine. They phoned us!'

When he was gone, Steve found Helena by his side, clutching his arm below the shoulder. Her eyes were wide, her face tense and pale. He felt everybody in the room looking at him. What were they seeing?

'Are you all right?' she said. 'God, that was scary. Would you really have hit him? I've never been anywhere near a fight before. You might have been terribly hurt.' She seemed to be controlling tears, as she continued, 'Jim Kearney's a disgrace, a horrible man. The university ought to be rid of him.'

'But it's run by men,' said Jan, who had followed Helena.

Still holding on to him Helena turned to Jan, but then Catherine came to kiss his cheek, saying, 'Steve saved the situation. Don't you all see? Who knows what might have happened if Jim Kearney had kicked that man in the heart, or in the head! We were all standing around, helpless. There were men behind Jim who could have grabbed him and held him back. Steve got it under control. I thought he was going to kill that man. I've never seen such hatred in anyone's eyes.'

'Thanks, mate,' Mike said, bringing a beer. 'It's a good job you were here. I'd have had to tackle him myself.' Then, with a rueful smile, 'I might well have lost.'

'Good job he didn't see me coming,' Steve said, glad of Mike's approach. 'I wonder if he'll use the sports centre again.'

'I think he will, though he could turn nasty. He could have been looking at GBH, or worse. I'll make sure I speak to him; try to make him see he should be grateful to you, even if he doesn't actually let you know.''

Mike led Steve into the kitchen, where Catherine was preparing him a plate of cold meat, home-made quiche, and salad.

Accepting the plate, Steve looked again, as if to find his bearings, at the electrical sockets, the cooker and washing machine he'd installed. People came up to him and said 'Well done.'

Max said, 'Now you see why you always have some space when we're playing five-a-side.'

Meanwhile there was a buzz of conversation about Kearney.

'He's the very model of a phoney sociologist.'

'All his research into the debts of the poor and how they spend their money - bollocks about the obvious.'

'Amazingly successful at securing research grants.'

'He probably wouldn't have harmed Denise's new man.'

'Playground stuff really. Handbags at ten paces.'

Accompanying these remarks, Steve was aware of wary looks at himself, as if he'd caused the trouble and might cause some more. What would he have done, if Kearney had sprung up at him? Was he primed to fight Kearney because of Kearney's campaign about the sports centre, and about the O'Kanes; and about the way Kearney had looked at Helena? Was he a Dumbo Rambo? Did Helena need him now as much as he needed her?

She was talking to Jan, who had kept her in the lounge. Jan was blocking the door to the kitchen with her back to him, so Helena could only look at him over Jan's head. It was as if a separation from Helena he'd been feeling all night, as she mingled in her academic world, was being confirmed. More than ever he was convinced Jan was hostile to him, believing a beautiful intelligent woman like Helena was wasted on him.

But eventually, as the party came to an end, he decided he didn't care what had happened. Helena had chosen him. He'd turned down some good looking women.

And back in his house, after Helena and he had walked home down the Whitstable Road hand in hand, he definitely didn't care.

In his bedroom they undressed each other slowly, their hands lingering where each knew the other was dying to be touched.

In bed she rolled him onto his back and knelt astride him, his hands naturally reaching up to her lovely breasts, before sliding all over her body.

'*Before, behind, between, above, below,*' she sighed smilingly, her eyes closing with pleasure.

'You're quoting something even now,' he accused her, his own voice husky with passion.

'I know, but the words are so true, and I want you so much.'

IX

'This square's too good to be true, except it's crammed with parked cars,' Theresa announced to Pat. 'Talk about picture-postcard - castle at one corner, church opposite at another; pub, cottages with roofs all shapes, tea-room!'

Just after ten on the May Sunday morning they were strolling into the village square of Chilham, near Canterbury. They had walked up the hill from the official car park and were making their way to the church, the path to which was guarded by the White Horse pub.

'Feed the body as well as the soul,' Liam had said to Theresa, when they'd had a drink at the White Horse a couple of Sundays ago.

Today she and Pat were in Chilham to sign in for the area's annual 'Churches Walk', a circuit of about fourteen miles, beginning and ending at any one of the five churches taking part. They didn't intended a complete circuit, but only a short stretch from Chilham, along the North Downs Way, to Boughton Aluph church. Liam had been called up to London, leaving Theresa alone in Wye with Sunday on her hands. On edge from lack of action, and seeing the walk advertised, she'd contacted Pat. This morning he'd driven over from Faversham. They'd met at Boughton Aluph church, where they'd left Pat's Marina. Then they'd driven in Theresa's Cortina to the car park at Chilham.

Inside the church they queued to sign in at the desk immediately inside the nave, Theresa as Maddie Warren, Pat as Thomas Pike. Asked for their donation and where it should go, they each gave five pounds and named Kent Air Ambulance.

'Old church,' Theresa observed to the woman behind the desk.

'Fifteenth century some of it,' she replied. Then, handing over stick-on badges and cards to be signed at each church, 'Done the walk before?'

'First time; we're only in Kent for the weekend,' Theresa replied. 'Visiting friends in Ashford.'

Outside they crossed the square and began their route by descending the lane alongside the village's Jacobean castle. Other groups and couples were also starting at Chilham, but they would soon be separated according to their different speeds.

'Best for us to give money to the air ambulance,' Pat remarked. 'Even we might need it, if something went wrong.'

'Better than giving money to a church we might blow up,' Theresa responded.

'Nothing for us in destroying a village church. Anyway Liam wouldn't let you do it. He was going to be a priest, remember.'

'He never lets me forget.'

They soon reached the end of the metalled road descending alongside the castle grounds. Shortly the open countryside of the Stour valley was before them with a view of Godmersham Park and its eighteen century stately home. Theresa was relying on the specially erected signposts for the walk, but in the church at Chilham Pat had bought a map.

Stopping and consulting the map, he said, 'Let's miss Godmersham church. It's like an extra loop. If we go to it, we've only got to come back again to join the North Downs Way.'

'C'mon,' Theresa urged. 'That's a bit wimpy! We're not doing much of the walk as it is. There's cakes and stuff at every church. We can eat some at Godmersham and fuel up for Boughton Aluph.'

'I'm telling you, Godmersham church is out for me; not with the climb the North Downs Way takes, when we come back to it.'

Sensing he wouldn't change his mind, Theresa looked hard at Pat, noticing again how he hardly seemed to contact the physical world, always seemed to be existing apart from it; unlike Sean and Matthew, who filled their days working for O'Connor's road-laying gangs.

'Whatever you like,' she said eventually. 'We'll just walk a short distance towards the house to have a better view of it.'

But when they returned and began the climb up the North Downs Way to King's Wood, he couldn't stay with her. She had to keep stopping to wait for him, only to have him immediately drop yards behind her as soon as they started again. At the top of the climb, he demanded they rest on a stile, while he took a drink from his bottle of water.

'This is all getting too much for me,' he said, after some minutes silence.

'Getting too much? What's getting too much?'

'This business we're in, killing people, never ending war till Ireland's united.' Taking another drink of water, he declared, 'It's never going to happen, and we're missing everything.'

'Missing everything?'

'Life. We're missing life.'

Theresa looked with him into the distance, down the hill they'd just climbed. From their resting place on the stile, Godmersham Park and its great house looked as though they had belonged to the Stour valley forever.

'In bed with Guy Portway,' Pat said, his eyes closing, as if to re-enter the experience, 'if we could have gone somewhere, anywhere, away from everything … ;' he didn't finish.

Guy Portway, Theresa thought. They'd all known his first name, but she'd never heard any of them use it before. She wondered if she could have shot him if she'd ever called him Guy.

'I've never known how you feel about me for killing the captain,' she said, eventually. 'Liam thought you might lose it altogether. He was ready to have you eliminated.'

Pat drank some more water.

'I'll tell you now,' he said. 'When we made that trip to Deal to recce that music school, you were close to death yourself on Ramsgate station. I was ready to push you under a train.'

'So why didn't you?'

'Admiration.'

'Admiration?'

'Weird, I know. That you could be so cold, killing a man up close like that; something I've never done. Closing yourself off to all feelings. You were what I once thought I wanted to be - absolute.'

If only, she thought.

'I've done more than fifteen years in this game,' Pat declared. 'I was carrying messages as a boy, guns sometimes. Once you're in, how do you get out? How do you get back to normal - loving someone? How do you say all you've done was a waste of your life?'

'Jesus, you're trapped like Liam, like the O'Kanes. We're all trapped. We're just pawns in our own lives!'

Another group was approaching. They got down from the stile, so the group, four adults, three children, could pass when it arrived.

When they were again on their own and continuing the walk themselves, Pat said, as if to explain everything, 'Guy Portway, you know, was so vulnerable. He couldn't even tell his parents he was gay.'

Getting no response, he added, in resignation, 'We're all vulnerable.'

'But you've got a lot of credit coming to you from that trip we both made to the Marines School of Music in Deal,' Theresa insisted. 'Liam tells me it's being seen as an easy target, and we found it. You could use it to bargain yourself free.'

'Yeah,' Pat said, unconvinced.

Almost immediately they were now alongside King's Wood and its silent sea of bluebells, motionless under the gloom of its trees; the densest, largest spread of the flowers Theresa had ever seen, the perfume heavy, drug-like.

Sister O'Leary, who'd wanted her to go to university, came immediately into her head, reading to the class, 'One of my favourite poems.'

What was that line? Yes, 'The woods are lovely, dark, and deep.' Wasn't there snow in the poem? No snow here, but looking into the woods from the May sunshine, they were lovely, dark, and deep, their bluebells magical, inviting you to enter and escape. No men, no IRA, no troubles ever again.

'Jesus!'

The woods passed, the path descending, Boughton Aluph church in sight, Pat had stumbled.

'I've done my ankle in.'

He sat at the side of the path, groaning, taking his boot and sock off.

'Now what can we do?' she asked. She was suddenly fed up with Pat.

'Rest a bit.' Irritated, he stood up, seeing if his bare foot could carry any weight, 'Oh!'

Great baby, she thought. You're supposed to be terrorising the Brits.

A man and a woman approached, 'Five Churches' badges stuck on their jackets. Her heart leapt. It was the man, and the woman, she'd seen in the cathedral at the site of Becket's tomb!

'Problem?' the man asked.

'Done my ankle in,' Pat said.

'Have you got anything for it, bandage?'

'Nothing at all.'

'Want me to have a look?'

'He knows about sports injuries,' the woman said. 'He runs the sports centre at Canterbury University.'

Crouching at the side of the path, the man was opening his rucksack. He took out an aerosol and some bandages. Theresa watched him kneel down close to Pat and tenderly run his fingers over Pat's bare ankle. She wished it was her ankle.

'I'm Steve, by the way,' he said. 'This is Helena. We're doing the walk, like you.'

'We're only doing a short bit,' Theresa said. 'Chilham to Boughton Aluph. We've a car at Boughton Aluph.'

'We're going all the way round, back to Chilham,' the man said. 'I've just been hearing all about Jane Austen visiting her brother at Godmersham Park. That slowed us down a bit. Helena teaches literature.'

'Everything's a race to Steve,' the woman said, smiling.

'I'm Maddie,' Theresa said. 'This is Tom.'

'I'm going to use this cold spray,' the man said, nodding at them both to acknowledge their names. 'It'll help control the swelling, take the heat out. It might not be a good idea to spray it directly onto the skin, so I'll spray it through this tissue.'

He sprayed the ankle carefully.

'That should start to feel better,' he said to Pat after he'd finished. 'I've seen a lot worse.'

'He was in the army,' the woman said.

'We're very grateful,' Theresa responded.

'Yeah,' Pat added. Standing up, he tried some weight on the ankle. 'That's a lot better.'

'I'm going to do a bandage to give you some support,' the man said. 'You should easily make it to Boughton Aluph. You can have the stick I picked up to lean on.'

Theresa watched him skilfully bandaged Pat's ankle. When he looked up, she had her eyes ready to gaze into his.

'I've seen you before,' he responded with a grin.

'In the cathedral.'

'That's it, when Helena was reading about Becket. She's always reading to me.'

'Thanks, Steve,' the woman said.

'No. I enjoy it. Really.' To Theresa he said, 'She told me baddies used to hide in King's Wood and attack pilgrims on their way to Becket's shrine.'

Soon everything was finished. With his boot back on, Pat stood up and walked a bit, using the stick the man gave him. 'You're a miracle worker,' he said to the man.

'Just glad to help. But we'd better be moving on. We've a long way to go.'

He packed up his rucksack and arranged it on his back.

Another group of walkers was passing.

'We'll say *Au Revoir* then,' the woman said.

Nods and smiles, as they left, Theresa watching the woman move close to the man, so he could put his arm around her, pull her close, and kiss her forehead, and so she could kiss his cheek. There's a man to go anywhere with, she thought.

'Well, well, well,' Pat mocked. 'Now it's our Theresa's turn to fall for the enemy.'

X

'Come on! Give it to me! Give it to me hard! Push h-a-r-d! H-A-R-D!'

'Is that sex, or is one of them giving birth?' Yatesy asked Steve. 'It's a bugger to listen to.'

The middle of a June afternoon in the fitness suite at the sports centre. Two men were bench-pressing in the weights area, one of them bending demandingly over the other. On the bench the man lifting hissed through clenched teeth, his eyes closed tight, his face knotted in a passionate grimace. Moaning, sighing, even whimpering, he straightened his arms and forced the barbell onto its stand. Then he lay collapsed on his back, arms dangling to the floor, mouth falling open, eyes now softly closed. Spent.

Could be after sex, Steve thought, or dead.

He was helping Yatesy who was also bench-pressing.

'Health and safety,' he'd insisted, when Yatesy said he'd be OK on his own. 'Anyway, it gives me a chance to be in there and see what's going on, without looking as if I'm on patrol.'

Later he was going for a run with Helena and Mike Connery; so while Yatesy did some other lifts with his usual massive ease, he stretched hamstrings, calves, groins.

'You're going to shag yourself out,' Yatesy said, as he did a series of powerful, lateral-raises, simultaneously lifting both arms sideways from his hips till the heavy dumbbell in each hand was level with his shoulders, like a mighty crucifix.

Bloody difficult that, Steve thought, admiringly.

The two men bench-pressing had changed places. Now the one doing the encouraging was more coaxing. 'E-a-s-y, e-a-s-y,' he was saying soothingly to his friend. 'You know you can do it.'

The whole room was full of people purposely going through various programmes. Several women were there, feeling confident they could now enter a space in the sports centre that used to be a grim retreat for men. Steve had had it painted in appealing colours and bought in new sets of weights that began right down the scale. There were machines for all kinds of lifting and pulling, and for cycling, rowing, walking, skiing; equipment for inner and outer thighs; simple broomsticks for twisting exercises. He wanted the fitness suite to be for anybody wanting to keep in shape, healthy; not just for body-builders.

After Yatesy had showered, they sat in the coffee bar, another of Steve's innovations.

'This is what you call a "real earner",' he said. 'It's becoming a social meeting place. For a lot of students it's as far as they ever come into the sports centre.'

'You can't make them keep fit,' Yatesy said. 'And you're like me; you need to make money. Your job depends on it. Don't listen to anybody who wants you to do things where there'll be no take-up. We have this all the time, folks asking us why we don't hold stuff we know we'll never sell. Most people have no idea about running a business.'

Steve had been telling Yatesy that earlier in the day he'd met a delegation of women students from the Students' Union.

'Why has this sports centre never had a woman as director, or even assistant director,' they'd complained. 'The only women are receptionists and your secretary.'

He'd told them he was advertising for a woman assistant director very soon, and the coffee bar was helping to pay for it.

'You've your perfect number here, Stevey,' Yatesy said. 'You're in shorts or tracksuits all day; Helena's fifteen minutes' walk away. Some of us have to work for a living.'

Helena might soon be thousands of miles away, Steve thought, knowing the decision on keeping her for another year at

Canterbury was pending, and that she now had a real chance of moving to America. But all he replied was, 'You enjoy what you're doing.'

'Yeah, I do,' Yatesy said. 'It keeps me out and about, meeting people, town planners, even archaeologists on some sites. I like mucking in with the lads, when we're taking something down, and I can usually make time to stop off and see Carol, or come here. My dad's having a bit of bother, though, selling the breakers' yard. People who staked him want a cut. They're at death's door some of them, in nursing homes, having to be fed with a spoon, but they won't bleeding let go. Twenty, thirty years after their life of crime, they never forget. They hold on to grudges about who got what in the jobs they did; who did time in jail; who didn't.' Then, when Steve didn't reply, 'It's made me think again about the O'Kanes and the photos in the papers. Somebody's not forgotten them. What if there was a grudge against us?'

'Who knows we were involved?' Steve said. 'I've told you. We carry on as if it never happened.'

Yatesy left, and Steve had some work to do before Helena and Mike turned up. He wanted to do the calculations again about employing an assistant director: what the coffee bar would earn, money he could squeeze from other sources, charges he could raise. Last Sunday the sports centre had had an 'Open Day' for families, another of his initiatives. It let people know what the centre offered, gave them a chance to use some of the equipment for free.

He'd enjoyed seeing them park their cars and walk the last fifty yards or so in the early June sunshine with their children. Couples held hands, some giving each other a happy kiss. The centre attracted over thirty family subscriptions, and the barbecue made a ton of money, thanks to Yatesy wangling him a deal on meat from an old school mate. There was some aggro: dads at each other's throats during the junior five-a-side tournament, sports centre regulars pissed-off because they had to queue a bit longer for the equipment. Some of these dozy sods still hoped he'd make a balls-up, because they wanted to believe the charges were all his doing. They thought they could get back to when everything was free, as if the money used to come from nowhere! 'Why don't they cut defence spending?' a young academic yelled at him. He'd be the kind of bastard who went around muttering, 'He was just a squaddie before he came here,' the kind who talked a lot about democracy, but wanted everybody to think the same way.

Steve knew Jim Kearney was still an enemy, looking for revenge after Mike Connery's party, trying to rile him, hoping he'd step out of line, even be sacked. Last week he was waiting for Helena in his running things, when Kearney walked past with a squash partner and said, so he could hear,

'Here's a bought and sold long distance runner, anything but lonely.'

Bound to be an insult, though he didn't understand it.

Then, looking back over his shoulder, Kearney sneered, 'Your juicy young Shirley Williams, no problem for a Tory like you. She'll ditch Labour when the workers want too much.'

He might have chinned Kearney, if Helena hadn't appeared from the women's changing rooms.

'What's going on?' she asked.

'Nothing,' he said.

But it was all clear today, as he met Helena and Mike at the sports centre entrance, changed and tanned, and ready for eight miles.

'Easy this afternoon, so we can talk,' Mike declared, as their digital stop-watches began racing the micro-seconds away. 'But not more than fifty-six minutes.' All three knew they could beat fifty-six minutes for eight miles whenever they wanted to, even in the heat.

Passing the house at the top of Rough Common Road, where Steve now knew Virginia Woolf had stayed and written, 'There is no lovelier place in the world than Canterbury', they were soon on the narrower shaded paths of the woods, Helena and Mike side by side, Steve behind, loving the swish of Helena's hair as it fanned out from the tight elastic band at the back of her head, and listening to them discussing Helena's career prospects.

'You could come back from Rocky Mountains University,' Mike was saying. 'English is nearly guaranteed a permanent job next year, and everybody would want you.'

'Maybe,' Helena responded. 'But RMU is sounding serious. They're interested in all my stuff about writers and places. They want to set up a data base, and I've already got a lot of the data.'

Steve had already had this direct from Helena. It was churning him up.

Then they started talking about Emily Dickinson. Mike had read Helena's thesis when Helena applied for the job at Canterbury, and now the thesis had just been published as a book. A poem about a 'loaded gun' was mentioned. Steve heard Helena say the gun was 'figurative.'

'This is all shop,' Mike admitted, looking back to Steve.

'Usually is with academics,' Steve responded

Helena turned her head sideways, sticking out her tongue at him.

Oh, that tongue. Don't leave me.

Now they were running through a quiet valley, along a hot unshaded macadam road, the light so sharp and clear it magically foreshortened the distances to cottages and farmhouses on the hillsides.

'Garden of England!' Helena exclaimed excitedly, gesturing to the abundant hedgerows. 'Hawthorn, quick-thorn, greater celandine, dog roses, cow parsnip, honeysuckle, spear thistle. Get to know the world, everybody!'

As usual they speeded up for the last quarter of a mile and were going flat out for the final two hundred yards, Mike forging ahead, Helena and Steve side by side. As they slowed to a halt on the forecourt of the sports centre, she put a hand on his bicep and kissed his cheek.

After they had all showered and changed, Steve and Helena waved Mike on his way home and then walked to her car parked near the English department. The Renault Five started first time.

'New plugs, points and condenser,' Steve said from the passenger seat. 'Get to know your world, Helena.'

Turning towards him, she mouthed a kiss, making a gentle popping sound as her lips parted.

XI

'God, I'm ready for this,' Helena said an hour later, towards seven o'clock, grabbing a beer from Steve's hand and sitting at his kitchen table; 'after all the water I've drunk.'

'Spaghetti and meat sauce à la Catherine,' he announced, putting a plate of food before Helena before sitting down to his own plate. 'She showed me how to reduce the sauce till it's really rich. I made it yesterday, so all the flavours have had a chance to mingle.'

'I hope you weren't too bored by all that talk on the run,' Helena said, forking up some spaghetti. 'It's just that I've hardly seen Mike since my Dickinson book was published. He wanted to tell me how much he was enjoying it.'

'That must have been good to hear. But why couldn't Emily Dickinson write so people could understand her? Couldn't she make her mind up? And what's all that about a loaded gun? You've mentioned it before.'

'Like a lot of Dickinson's poems this particular poem's mysterious,' Helena responded. 'Feminists often interpret it as saying something about women and their violation by men, but I think the poem's bigger than that. I argue it's about what it's like to be a human being, man or woman. I actually think gender references in the poem could be swapped for their opposite (male for female and vice versa), and the poem would still make complete sense.'

'I heard Mike say feminists were keeping him out of the poem, but you were letting him back in.'

'The poem's first line is, 'My Life had stood - a Loaded Gun -'. Among other possible meanings I think the poem's about an overwhelming potentiality that might be latent in anyone's life, man or woman. The potentiality might never be released, and you could live out your days undisturbed by it. Alternatively, it might be triggered. Then it might violently, destructively, possess you.'

'My life had stood a loaded gun,' Steve echoed; 'sounds like something a terrorist might say, an IRA sniper. But is the poem claiming we're not responsible for our own lives? Is that what you think?'

'Your sniper interpretation's good,' Helena replied, drinking more beer. 'Imagine the first time an assassin has the weapon handed to him or her, and the victim assigned – a moment that might never have happened, but is life-changing when it does. As for your question, I'm not deterministic or fatalistic, but we are, and we aren't, responsible for our lives.'

Sprinkling more grated parmesan onto her food, she continued, 'You're born into a life that's given to you by some energy or force or whatever. You don't immediately choose your life. You're not presented with alternatives. Choice and responsibility come later, but there's always the history you inherit without your say-so, a history which might hand a loaded gun to you; then there's developments in your life you can do nothing about. As for getting what you deserve, that may have little to do with anything.' Pushing the parmesan back towards him, 'That's one reason I'm a member of the Labour Party - to avoid too much self-congratulation, to try to spread good luck around, or at least compensate for people's bad luck.'

No politics, Helena, not now, he thought.

Then he said, 'I suppose you think I make my own way too much, but it's just that I've always felt I had to. Even if I'd stayed on at school it would have been the same. I always feel it's down to me - always. It's why I fix things myself; my car, your car; apart from saving the money. I think I should tackle any job myself. I left school because I thought if I had to make my own way I must do what I really wanted to in a world I could control, and that was play for United.'

'And in no time at all you were trying to control the world with a loaded gun in your hands. So was the gun always waiting for you?'

When he didn't answer, Helena quoted: 'For I have but the power to kill, / Without - the power to die –'.

'These are the last two lines of the poem,' she said. 'The speaker (let's assume it's female) feels her life's energy has become entirely murderous, out of harmony with all things - with life and with death. Perhaps your friend Maurice Sims shot himself to reclaim the power to die, and therefore to re-claim ultimate control of his life. But the appalling paradox was that this could only be done by an act of self-murder, so maybe Dickinson means something else by "the power to die"; maybe it's the power finally to relinquish power, because together your life and death make sense for you, complete you.'

'How could you ever know?'

'Big question.'

There was silence while they each mopped up the meat sauce with pieces of bread. But then he had to bring it out into the open. He'd go crazy if it wasn't sorted.

'What's going to happen to us, Helena?'

She drained the rest of her beer from the bottle.

'Steve, I'm not intending to draw a line under anything with you and me, but, I can't have no job. The academic profession's like every other. You're either on the inside, or you really don't count. People forget about you, and you're stuck with an obsolete CV.'

'What about my job, my career, my CV?'

'I don't know. But I don't want our relationship to end.'

'How can it go on, you over there, me here?'

Reaching her hand across the table to rest it on his, she said, 'I'm not over there yet, but there's a good chance. One of the publisher's readers who recommended publication of my Dickinson book runs literature at RMU. If I got the job, we could try things at long range, like other people facing our kind of problem. I can come and see you here. You can come and see me there.'

I have to see more of you than that, he thought.

'If I establish myself,' she continued, as if sensing his thought, 'you may want to come and join me, permanently. Steve, that's what I'd really like, and it's not that you'd be stuck for something to do. You won't want to hear this, but you could even go "back to school", as they say in the States, full-time if you want to. I've plenty of money from my mother. But I do want to work. I must work.'

'So it's me who'd have to give things up for you,' he said, 'leaving my job to be a student at my age.'

As he served them both some salad, he imagined his brother's reaction. Gordon was over the moon when he became director of the sports centre and was settling down to a proper job. But Gordon's wife would support him, and their sister. They'd been behind him when he went to United. Funny how women could be more up for things, as if they wished they were making the move themselves. He'd have to sell the Jag.

'Why should it always be a woman giving up her job for a man,' Helena asked, breaking off some more bread for herself, 'living off a man? Think of it as another new opportunity, something positive. We're both still young. You'd love the Rockies. You're made for physical adventure.'

'I need time to get my head round all this,' he answered, even as he felt a great surge of happiness. She wanted him to be with her, for the long run!

The salad finished, she stood up to clear the table and make the coffee, something she usually did when he cooked. But first of all she came to sit on his knee, putting her arms round his shoulders and then his neck, her breasts pushing softly into his face. Kissing his forehead, she said, 'The poem about the loaded gun is at best tragic, at worst bleak. And even if it is about masculine systems perverting women's lives, it doesn't apply to you, nor to all men. Women impoverish life in thinking so. I'd love to have you with me in the States. What more can I say to you?'

But a few minutes later, standing with her back to the sink, waiting for the kettle to boil, and perhaps speaking as much to herself as to him, she declared, 'I recognise feminists say some way-out things. I've just been reading an American article which claims that because women tend to marry older men, they're always marrying a version of their father, and therefore heterosexual marriages are incestuous. Who knows where that leaves real victims of incest?'

Spooning coffee into the cafetière (too much, Steve thought), she declared, 'Anyway it's not these extreme views that are the problem. It's the every-day assumptions in the working world. Even the unions are complicit in a prejudice against women that's like racial prejudice. You wouldn't know it, but we've had an equal pay act since nineteen seventy-five! All that's happened is that jobs have been segregated, with women doing the ones that are worst paid. Almost the entire university's cleaned by women. Imagine it the other way round, if you as a man saw men always doing the jobs people have the least respect for; on their knees, like the woman I saw today polishing a great brass plant-holder in the so-called atrium. Wouldn't you feel at least indignant?'

Pouring water into the cafetière and putting some milk on the stove to warm, she didn't wait for his answer.

'I went to the Edinburgh Festival last summer. One of the acts on the Fringe was a woman comedian, part of whose act was blatant self-abuse. She was grossly fat, hair like tangled barbed wire, studs in her nose and tongue, and lots of hints about metal in more intimate parts of her body. It was as if she was saying, "I'll violate myself first before anyone else has the chance". As she came on, her first words were, "Don't worry, I'm not about to have a baby. Who'd want to have sex with me?".

'Why should any woman feel she needs to be like that? Why has our woman prime minister only ever appointed one woman to her cabinet and has none in it now? Is it because she too has little respect for her own gender? As for women in the university's senior management, there aren't any. And women professors, they must be outnumbered by men at least ten to one! English is full of women students, but nearly all their teachers are men.'

She pressed the plunger of the cafetière too vigorously causing coffee and grains to shoot over the top. Coffee's ruined, Steve thought, but Helena mopped up the mess, as if it always happened when you made coffee.

Like a bell bringing to end a round of boxing, in which Steve felt he'd been backed up into his corner, the phone rang. When Steve answered, it was Gordon wanting to talk about their dad's health, which Steve already knew was getting worse. Emphysema had been a problem for well over a year, but now a cancer on his dad's lungs was eating his dad away.

Still looking unsettled, Helena gave Steve his coffee and signalled she would go upstairs. She often used the tiny second bedroom as a study.

Listening to Gordon giving what reassurance he could, Steve visualised his dad to a soundtrack from his childhood. He'd seen his dad a fortnight ago when Helena had gone to Oxford to visit her father. At only sixty-five he looked an old man, poisoned by the diesel fumes and fags (thousands of his own) that had been his working life as a bus conductor ever since the war.

'In t'garage,' he used to say, 'first thing in a mornin'; all th'engines startin' up, and then t' bus full o' pitmen and their smoke.'

Before the clean air act he'd walked in front of his bus with a lamp, showing the driver the way through filthy Lancashire fogs.

'Knackered all over,' he'd announce, when he got home.

And sometimes half-laughing at himself, 'When I come out of th'army, I vowed I'd never wear a uniform again, an' I wore a bus conductor's uniform for nearly forty years.'

To which his wife would respond, 'One good thing about your job, it provides you with clothes.'

Ordinary, basic jobs, Steve thought, as he washed up after the phone call, and then shoved Helena's and his pricey running gear into the washing machine. Working men as well as Helena's working women - they've got the power to kill all right, the power to kill themselves, the power to work themselves to death, like my dad.

Helena came down in time for *Newsnight* on TV, and Steve watched it with her without paying much attention. Since the miners' strike he'd sometimes found the programme to be like *Match of the Day* - edited highlights of punch-ups between miners and coppers, with a commentary on who kept it tight, who was looking to mix it, who went over the top.

On the screen a face appeared he was sure he recognised. It was a photograph of a handsome young man, square-jawed, clean cut, not a hair out of place, like someone advertising hair products or shaving gear. Then viewers were shown a man and a woman seated in the studio in two easy chairs opposite an interviewer. The photograph was blown-up behind them.

The man and the woman (husband and wife in their fifties, respectable) were looking for their son. They were a major and Mrs Portway, and their son was Guy. The photograph was of him, and he too had been an officer in the army, a captain. He'd been missing for several months, however, and all his parents' inquiries about him were being deflected. Their MP was getting nowhere.

The interviewer went through the motions of interest and concern.

'And what you want from this programme is publicity for your campaign against the MOD's closed doors,' she said by way of conclusion.

'We want to know where our son is,' the mother insisted.

Suddenly Steve remembered, 'These two are special. ... Get them over to that captain who's just turned up in that Saracen.'

Jesus Christ, Captain Guy Portway was the officer Yatesy and him had handed the O'Kane brothers to!

'A very good-looking son,' Helena commented.

'I saw him in Northern Ireland,' Steve blurted out.

'What?'

Should he tell her? Wouldn't it be a relief to tell her, even if she wouldn't be satisfied with anything but the full story, so she'd have to know about his involvement with the O'Kanes? He couldn't lie to her. He never had.

'Me and Yatesy,' he said. 'We handed the O'Kanes over to that Captain Portway.'

'No!'

'We didn't know who he was at the time, and we've never seen him since, not till this photo on the telly.'

He described the supposed ambush of the IRA assassination squad in South Tyrone, the year before the Falklands War; the fire-fight, three of their own killed, five IRA dead, two IRA prisoners; Yatesy and him ordered to escort the two prisoners to an officer he now knew was Captain Guy Portway; his discovery from the photos published this year that the two prisoners were the O'Kane brothers who'd completely disappeared.

'Are you sure the officer was Captain Portway?'

'Positive. I knew it as soon as I saw his face on the telly.'

'But nobody can be sure about memory. We remember what we think we remember.'

'I'm telling you I don't forget faces; that Polish woman who was over here.'

'Maria Jarzebska from Krakow?'

'Whatever she was called. I saw her about twice and not for long. In a crowd I'd recognise her. That Captain Portway was the officer we handed the O'Kanes to.'

After a silence, he continued, like a confession, 'The O'Kanes had been beaten up by our lot, even though one of them was already badly wounded. Yatesy lost it, first time and never again. He'd been looking after one of our lads shot in the head. It was the lad's first tour.'

'What are you going to do?'

'What can I do, but keep quiet? The O'Kanes will have been killed, for sure; probably tortured first. I bet Portway's been killed too. The IRA must have found out about him. With the IRA we've people inside everything, and they've people inside everything.'

It came back to him: the night-time patrols, nearly shitting yourself, always on edge - a booby trap, a sniper's bullet.

'I hope Yatsey and Carol don't watch *Newsnight*,' he said. 'If we're exposed, Yatsey and me are next in line, and Carol's ready to have her baby. Killing us would be more revenge for the IRA, or cover your arse time for our lot, same difference.'

'A real heart of darkness.'

'What?'

'Nothing. You're right. Don't get involved. Don't let that conflict take hold of you again.'

He sat silently, more army life dragging him back despite what she said. His commanding officer, who'd done his reference for the sports centre, wanted him for the SAS.

'Look,' she interrupted. 'It's time I went home. You know I'm not staying the night.'

'Yeah, OK. I'll help you with your stuff.'

He was disappointed, but he knew she had exam scripts to read first thing. Earlier in the relationship he tried to change her mind when she said she was going back to her flat. If they were both turned-on she'd give in, but even then she might complain in the morning about not having her books around. 'I can't think without them.'

He helped her with her things to her car, and they hugged and kissed for longer than usual, before she slipped into the driver's seat and wound down the window.

'Surely what you've just learned is all the more reason to make a life together in the States,' she pleaded. 'That new world, you know, was created so people could forget the past.'

But watching her break lights blink on and off at the junction Steve was wondering if he was all that different from his dad after all. Had he ever had any more control over his own life than his dad had had over his?

XII

'The miners must be feeling crucified by debts,' Rick McKnight insisted to Charles Furlow.

The two of them were again in Furlow's office, Furlow folded into his chair behind his desk, McKnight seated opposite him, as if in an ejector seat about to thrust him out of the room.

'Why don't we have letters sent to the all the strikers,' McKnight continued, 'final demand notes for immediate money, or else; send a few big guys to knock on doors, posing as debt-collectors?'

'We don't know which debts they have.'

'No problem. Who's talking facts? We'll send Mickey Mouse demands for payments on their houses, cars, TVs, furniture, heating, lighting, water - anything! All the letters will look official: headings, account numbers and so on; real phone numbers for queries. It'll cause no end of grief, especially if some of our letters coincide with real demand letters. Wives will be begging their husbands to go back to work.'

'You're going too far. Unscrupulousness against enemies of the state, members of foreign embassies, suspected spies is one thing. These miners are British citizens, ordinary workers, with rights like the rest of us. Some of them have served in the armed forces, fought for our country.'

'But now they want to bring down a democratically elected government. Scargill's a communist in all but name, so it's like a threat from the USSR. We need every weapon. Look what we're already doing. Miners are being stopped from driving up and down the A1 M.'

'You're thinking like these bloody Americans!'

Here the exchange was interrupted by a knock on the door.

Returning to his own office, pissed off at the reception of his scheme, McKnight clung to his jubilation that Furlow was still out in the cold and not in on Vigilance, Minter's special task force. Two days ago McKnight had been called to a seminar with slides and flip charts. It was to prepare for the planned battle at Orgreave. He remembered walking to the room behind Minter and the CIA man who'd followed Minter from the States. He caught fragments of what the CIA man was saying.

'Nicaragua - Iran - Contras - hog-tied - Democrats sucking each other's dicks.'

What the hell was all this was about?

But then he heard Minter say to the CIA man, 'Your people will be glad we cleaned the unions out of GCHQ; some return for the money you're putting into surveillance over here, a first step, long overdue.'

No problem with this. McKnight was right behind Mrs Thatcher's bulldozing the unions out of GCHQ in February. Soviet stooges in the country's intelligence hub, Jesus! Might as well give the commies the keys to number ten!

Taking his seat in the seminar room, McKnight nodded knowingly as Minter laid it on the line. Moles were burrowing into all the major unions. Planted stories were exposing the NUM's so-called misuse of members' funds. A projector displayed compromising photographs of all sorts of union officials at various junkets, women young enough to be their daughters on their arms or at their tables. At Orgreave Vigilance would ensure violence. Soldiers would be in police uniforms with no numbers. The BBC had been reminded who controlled its purse-strings, and allies in other network newsrooms were on-side. TVs throughout the land and abroad would show striking miners as a menace to civilisation.

This is the real deal, McKnight thought, smacking his fist hard into his palm. On his own with Minter for a few minutes, he mentioned Guy Portway, whose father was stirring things up on TV and writing letters to *The Times* about his missing son. He was sure Minter appreciated somebody had to stay on Portway's case. The IRA cell couldn't be forgotten about just because that public school tosser had gone AWOL.

'You're clear we're relying on you and a squad of men at Orgreave,' Minter said. 'But you say you've two good men you can spare.'

Relied on by Minter! Encouraged to use his initiative! Why not start his two good men, Adrian and Tony, afresh in Sussex? See if they could pick up where Portway left off. Last news from Portway he had an IRA cell in his sights - then, nothing. Loser, like Furlow.

McKnight knew that after Cambridge Minter had won a prestigious university scholarship in the US and walked straight into a job with America's intelligence agencies. With his shambling walk he didn't look a leader, but it was rumoured that for over a dozen years he'd headed a US team tracking some of the UK's brightest and best: movers and shakers in the military, politics, universities, business, trade unions, the media. People were saying it was the team's job to use any means to anticipate and block off anti-Americanism, anything pro-Soviet. Money and sex eased people along a path of self-advancement and made sure the UK, America's unsinkable aircraft carrier, steered a true course.

Wanting to give his life a keen American edge (sharp clothes, high tech apartment, telling car and woman, wad of readies in his hip pocket), McKnight couldn't wait for this kind of work to come his way. Score big with the miners and the IRA, nobody at his level would be near him. He'd be Minter's 'kinda guy'!

Red-haired Judith Rae, he was certain, was out of it, still living at Greenham Common with its crazy women. In April she'd been evicted from the site, even burning her makeshift tent for the TV cameras. But all the women, and more, soon came back. Now she was stirring up the locals against the protesters. Buying her round like a bloke at *The True Compass*, she'd described how two of her team, looking like witches from hell, knocked on the doors of people living near the airbase, asking if they could use the bog and have a bath.

'Good for a laugh, Judith, but you need some results and quick,' McKnight remembered saying to her.

Leaving his office three hours after Furlow's rejection of his latest plot against the miners, he wished he was already at Orgreave, though he'd be there in two days. His squad was already in the area, posing as miners, getting the feel. They had an assigned bunch of coppers from Essex to rumble with right in front of where the cameras would be positioned, coppers paid extra in cash on top of their official overtime money. He'd met an off duty chief superintendent in a pub in Chingford, a fat bastard in his fifties.

'We want guaranteed action for all this,' he emphasised pushing a duffle bag stuffed with notes across the table, along with three hundred pounds in an envelope for the superintendent himself.

'You'll get it,' the superintendent replied, folding up a plan of the field where the battle was going to happen. 'My lads are already buying new cars, caravans, extending their houses. For them this strike's like a win on the pools.'

This afternoon some release, humping a bar-maid from West Bromwich in her attic room in a pub off St Martin's Lane, till she was due back downstairs behind the beer-pumps - Geraldine! The slag took everything he had, and he was sure she'd another hustler lined up for the night-shift. But on his way, walking round the fountains in Trafalgar Square, he literally bumped into Furlow! The dozy sod was dodging some Japanese, who were photographing one another and everything else in sight.

'I do beg your pardon.' Then, 'McKnight!'

He was with a stooping man his own age and a woman McKnight would have traded Geraldine for on the spot. She'd never have another man on night-shift.

'Well, fancy that,' Furlow continued. 'We've just been in the National Gallery for an hour.' He hesitated before doing the introductions. 'This is my friend Peter Edwards, and his daughter Helena. She's been our excellent guide to some of the paintings - Titian, Holbein.' To his companions he said, 'Rick McKnight, one of my colleagues.'

They shook hands, the man friendly enough (nothing on the line for him), the girl indifferently (what could he ever mean for her?).

'I'm having a walk,' he said.

'Good. We all need exercise,' Furlow replied. 'But we'd better be getting along. I might see you later.'

Nods all round as they parted, Furlow exclaiming to the other two, 'That distorted skull slashing across the bottom of *The Ambassadors*!'

McKnight tried his usual test - walk about thirty yards, turn round and look back. If the girl's done the same, there's a chance.

This girl hadn't. He was right. There'd been no connection. He never did make connections with girls like that. Watching them wait for the lights to change so they could cross the road to go down Whitehall, he saw the girl hold on to her father's upper arm, protectively; obviously a close relationship; like he hoped his own would have been with his mother and father, if his father had not bankrupted and killed himself and his wife. What did his father think was going to happen to him as an orphan, brought up by his aunt and uncle? Was that even a consideration? His aunt said he had no table manners. She made him, but not her own children, eat at the table with a book under each arm pit. If a book fell out, he had to miss his meal and go to his bedroom.

'What's the matter with you this afternoon!' Geraldine demanded, when he was eventually shunting into her. 'Lost interest?'

There must be something better than this, he thought desperately.

But two days later he put Geraldine's question to Maddie, who came up to Orgreave with him. In bed in their nearby hotel the night before the big event, she wouldn't submit, and he thought she was hating it; till she really did get away all right, better than he ever did; nothing like his own stressed shudders. Why couldn't women just service him, and not want anything themselves?

'You always make it happen for me,' Maddie whispered afterwards, her small light body lying, as always, half on top of him. 'It's the secret powerful world you come from.'

'Up here I'm in control.'

'And not in London?'

'Maybe. Depends what happens up here.'

'The miners? That's everything?'

'Not everything. Depends what you mean.'

She was keeping him waiting, as always; but then, when he was nearly going crazy, her hand began gently to stroke him again.

'And?' she said.

'And?'

'The miners - if they're not everything, what else?'

'Why the interest?'

'Just so I don't feel I'm nothing to you - coming, going; no hold on anything.'

'You come all right, and you're holding something now.'

'I don't mean that. Sometimes I feel I'm no more than a scrap of waste paper to you.'

'What do I know about you? You won't tell me.'

'Later, when I know you. I'll tell you everything.'

Oh, her fingers! Don't stop!

'Security,' he murmured, losing himself. 'IRA.'

'IRA - no!'

'Fighting danger everywhere. Lost a captain. Lost the cell he was onto - Oh! Ah! Ah! Ah!'

'Now you're coming good,' she sighed into his ear.

Next morning he left her in bed. He was lending her the BMW to go to Chatsworth. To-night she promised another big night, and then she would come back to London with him; move into his flat; always be there for him.

But climbing into one of the vans driven by his men, he knew there was a vicious conflict ahead to-day, something to outrage and appal the Prime Minister and the British public. His men were confident the scene was ready to explode. Already the miners were wounded and frenzied. That crazy bastard Scargill (calling a coal strike over the summer!) had led them to believe it was going to be like nineteen seventy-four under that loser Heath. They hadn't expected this kind of police organisation. Determined to stop lorries leaving the hated coke plant at Orgreave to fuel Mrs Thatcher's England, they didn't suspect they'd been deliberately corralled onto a battlefield. They didn't know the lorries driving through strike-torn South Yorkshire to Scunthorpe and Flixborough were a calculated provocation, which ignored easier ways of transporting coke, at least to Flixborough.

'Keep the trucks on these roads,' Minter had said at a Vigilance meeting, while tracing the routes on a map on a screen. 'And make sure the miners can find their way to Orgreave. Let's have plenty of signposts.'

This battle today, eighteenth June, nineteen eighty-four, was a pre-ordained turning point. Finish off the miners! Finish off the unions! Finish off the IRA!

The miners are in for a beating, McKnight thought, relishing the prospect and feeling anticipation rise among the media people, as he arrived at his vantage point. The media people too were here for a big event (some of the photographers to make their names in the colour supplements) and must have something happen. Trained and tooled up for confrontation for the best part of a year, and sweating in their riot gear in the hot sunshine, the police were lusting to take a swing, and behind them were mounted forces, cavalry. The issues forgotten, there was going to be a primitive battle, a trial of male strength in which McKnight knew his men had the advantage of a plot. Even if they were arrested by coppers different from the Essex mob, he'd provided enough false documents to litter a paper chase to nowhere.

'This is still a green and pleasant land,' the driver of his van had said wistfully, as he parked. 'We should have done better with it.'

But as McKnight smoothed the soft leather of his Jaeger jacket and watched the heavy lorries lumbering out of the grimy coke-plant through their massed police guard, he saw only another northern shit-hole. You'd be away from here, if you had any balls, like he might be away some day from the entire fucking UK chaos, Maddie or no Maddie. His cousin from Zimbabwe had been staying with him, encouraging him to, 'Come and hilp us control, Mugabe, our own blick Scorgill.'

Miners and coppers were now in each others' faces; miners swearing, even pleading, addressing coppers as 'comrades,' claiming their struggle, 'was every worker's struggle, a fight for jobs, communities, wives and kiddies.'

'Why are you treatin' us like enemies?'

'I fought in the Falklands.'

'Our taxes pay your fuckin' wages.'

'We're gettin' skint, and you're makin' a fortune.'

'We can't put food ont' table.'

'You're fucking scabs.'

'This is a police state.'

'You're treatin' us like blacks in South Africa.'

Heaving into the massed riot shields, they were beaten back with truncheons. Again and again, trying to reach the gates of the coking plant to stop the lorries leaving it, they smashed into their opponents. When their line was forced back, solitary miners would stand like maddened boxers in a no-man's land, threatening 'to take on any fuckin' one of you, you cunts.' Then they would be joined by another assault from their mates. Fists flew and truncheons cracked heads. Stones, bricks, bottles pelted the police. McKnight could see blood on both sides and on the faces of his own crew. On a TV monitor he saw a close-up of a miner lying unconscious and face-down, at the side of the battle. Arrested miners were being dragged past him to waiting police vans. 'It took fuckin' four of you,' one said, still wrestling and struggling, kicking at a policeman who was taking off his shoes to toss them away.

Then an extra current of excitement swept through the media people. Scargill was hurt!

'Big chief Scargill down,' McKnight said to himself triumphantly. 'Doesn't he know the Indians are always massacred?'

The miners, he was certain, were going to lose this battle, and the war. They'd never stop the lorries. They were outnumbered, out-smarted. But let them throw their bottles and stones, and set fire to portakabins, he thought with satisfaction. It's just what's needed for the cameras before the miners are reduced to a rabble; before we humiliate them, break them; till we can do what we like with them; till the bastards are begging for any job at any price we put their way.

And now, at just the right time, the police used the horses, galloping into the miners' ranks, scattering them, making miners run for their lives as if fleeing an invading army. Chasing policemen picked out isolated, exhausted stragglers and vented a day's rage on them. McKnight watched a newspaper photographer crouch on one knee to capture a policeman rhythmically beating a cowering miner. The truncheon flew high into the air and then came thrashing down till its victim was flat on the ground, his clasped hands covering the back of his bloodied head.

'A walkover,' McKnight said, turning to a fraught TV man with a clipboard.

'What the hell do you know?' the man exclaimed. 'Wait till you see the editing!'

McKight set off in the direction of the vans, along the road, past houses, over the railway bridge. Miners were hiding in gardens, scrambling in hundreds down the railway embankment and across the lines.

And then, just before he reached the vans, he bumped into Judith Rae. Her red hair longer than usual she was about to slide into the back seat of a black Rover - an official car and driver!

'Rick,' she said, standing up by the open door of the car, so the door was a kind of shield.

'Judith! What are you doing up here? Greenham Common closed down?'

'David wanted me here. He's decided Greenham Common's a low priority.'

McKnight registered the 'David'. He'd never been confident in addressing Minter by his first name.

'We're driving straight back to London,' Judith said. 'We left first thing.'

'I'm in a hotel,' he replied. 'See you tomorrow at HQ.'

In the vans his men were celebrating with beers all round.

'I creamed a copper,' one of them shrieked. 'My boot went straight into his nuts. If he has a lady, she'll live like a nun for weeks.'

'Send her my way.'

'No need. Tarts enough in Sheffield to-night.'

'Get me to my hotel,' McKnight said to the driver.

In the car park he checked the BMW. It was where he'd parked it, as if it hadn't been moved. In the bedroom Maddie's stuff was gone. No sign of her.

XIII

Lying beside a warm and deeply slumbering Helena at three in the morning in Lost Angel Canyon, Colorado, Steve accepted there would be little sleep for him that night. Big moments in his life always kept him awake, and during these ten days with Helena he'd told her he would resign from his job in Canterbury and join her for a new life at Rocky Mountains University. She'd already been at RMU for over three weeks, having come for the successful interview early in July and then stayed on to make some preparations for her new career. Steve had flown over to join her in her rented former mining cabin as soon as she had phoned him to say she'd got the job, and they were both flying back to Heathrow from Denver later today. He planned to resign in time to be in the States with Helena as soon as possible after the beginning of September, when she started teaching. Now he let his mind drift over the last couple of weeks, re-assured that he would later sleep all the better on the plane.

'Do you love Helena?' Yatesy had asked him over a pint in the Thomas Becket the day before he drove to Heathrow.

'I can't live without her.'

'Then live with her in America. What's stopping you? I'd do anything to be with Carol. We'll miss you, miss you both; but once we're settled with the baby, we'll come over for a holiday.'

'That would be great.'

Walking home from the Thomas Becket he'd been relieved Yatesy had still said nothing about Portway's parents being on TV. He and Carol probably hadn't seen *Newsnight* after all, and the story hadn't made any kind of a splash, just minor ripples deep inside the quality press. Even if Yatesy had seen the *Newsnight* programme, Steve had anyway become pretty sure he wouldn't have recognised Portway as the captain they'd handed the O'Kanes to. The two of them had only been in Portway's presence a couple of minutes, and Yatesy had no reason to get a fix on the captain. As for Portway himself, it was Steve's eye he caught, because he was the corporal.

A drink with Yatesy always gave him a re-charge, and he remembered how much he'd needed it the day before he left for Heathrow. Meeting Yatesy in the pub, he'd just returned from Atherstone. While Helena was in Colorado, he'd gone home, mainly to visit his dying dad.

He'd stayed in the small two bedroom end-terrace house his parents had inherited from his dad's mother and done up with the proceeds from their own poorer house. What a contrast with the so-called mining cabin, where he now lay so snugly with Helena. Isolated with only half a dozen other scattered and sought-after cabins in a spectacular setting in the mountains, it had been expertly modernised and extended. Each of its two bedrooms had an en-suite bathroom. The inviting living areas were supported by a high-tech kitchen, and a basement had been excavated for a den, exercise equipment, and utility space. Outside, verandas south and west gave on to the untouched wilderness.

Opening the bedroom curtains to the morning sun at his parents' house, Steve had looked down a short narrow back garden (fifteen feet long) across a back lane (ten feet wide) straight into the littered yard of a small dilapidated cotton mill, now used by a firm making dresses, blouses and shirts. Sitting with his dad on a bench that leaned against the back wall of the house, he could see through the factory windows and watch garments dancing on their hangers, as conveyor belts took them to be pressed and packaged. In the warm weather young women stood on the iron fire-escapes, enjoying a smoke and a cuppa during their break, and waiving at Steve and his dad.

'When I'm gone,' his dad muttered, 'they'll say: "You know that old bloke who used to sit there; he's dead".'

Atherstone to Colorado, Steve now thought; Atherstone to anywhere! Sitting with him, Steve had wondered how his dad could stand returning to the house where he'd been a child, as if the entire journey of his life was only from the single bedroom Steve now slept in to the double one at the front of the house. Adding to this sense of futility his dad's clothes hung loose, like clothes belonging to someone else, and emphysema hunched his shoulders high towards his ears, as if he was a helpless puppet with death tightening its invisible harness on him. Alongside him, and knowing he could pick him up like a bundle of sticks, Steve visualised sports centre regulars pounding treadmills, heaving weights, driving themselves hard in aerobics - all of them intending to dominate their bodies, deny age, deny death.

Thank God his sister-in-law had cheered him up, telling him excitedly, when he spoke of Colorado, 'You'll be way out West.'

Gordon, though, had been gloomy, maybe because he knew the burden of their dad's death would fall mainly on him.

'I hope you know what you're doing,' he challenged Steve, before asking, 'will you be getting married?'

In bed with Helena Steve smiled to himself. To become a primary school headmaster after his non-graduate teacher training, Gordon had pushed himself through an Open University degree, while he was working. After all this effort Steve knew Gordon was amazed, and maybe also envious, that his younger brother, who'd left school to become a footballer, might now be on his way to the States with a young woman who had a first class Oxford degree and a Cambridge PhD, a woman wanting to become a professor at an American university!

He'd be even more wonderstruck, Steve knew, to hear this same young woman say to his brother in Colorado, 'I'll stake you for whatever you want to do.'

When Helena said this, they'd been looking at accommodation she might rent or buy nearer to RMU and more accessible in winter than the mining cabin. The experience gave Steve his first real sense of how much money Helena could actually lay her hands on. Obviously money answered questions, made things possible, especially, it seemed to Steve, here in this new world, where he was already beginning to recognise that what mattered most in your dealings with it was could you pay the bill; not where you came from, or what you sounded like, or who your parents were, but did you have the money. With Helena in his life Steve was becoming aware the answer would always be 'Yes,' and this left him feeling more liberated during these ten days than ever before in his life. In shops his Northern accent actually thrilled people, so much so they held him in conversation, spoke of their own holidays in England, Scotland and Ireland, and of family they had in these places.

'Have a nice day,' they said as he left, and he was convinced they meant it.

'It's an American custom all over the States,' Helena informed him, 'like the French *Bonne journée*, and here I've actually heard a man on the street selling vegetables refer to them as *légumes*, though he did pronounce the final consonant.'

She'd been to the States once before, four years ago, studying at the University of Massachusetts to help her PhD on Emily Dickinson. From there she'd flown with some friends for a stay in California, 'soaring over,' as she put it, 'the great central land mass of the continent.'

'The next few years will be hard for me too,' she'd insisted, three days into his stay, when, over lunch in a Mexican restaurant, he'd told her he'd leave Canterbury and join her in Colorado. He'd accompanied the announcement by exaggerated groaning over the possibility of becoming a student at RMU, something he saw as very different from the part-time degree he'd been accepted for in London. That would have run alongside the status of his sports centre job, a combination that now wouldn't happen for him.

'To get tenure and make this appointment permanent,' Helena continued, 'I need to write another book, and soon. So, you see, we can prove ourselves together. I'm going to write a book about "Literature and Place".'

He thought he sensed her becoming as relaxed as himself in this laid-back western world, and he was over the moon to see her so thrilled that he would be joining her for a new life. Striking miners and handing over the O'Kanes to Captain Guy Portway were thousands of miles away. Hadn't she said America was created, 'so you could forget the past'? Wasn't she right?

But then, always so responsive to experience, she struck a different note. It was two days after the lunch, when they took a three-day trip in her rented car to the *Mesa Verde National Park*, nearly four hundred miles south-west of Denver. There they explored the dwellings of some of America's aboriginal Puebloan people, Steve wondering if he'd ever seen anything that so completely overturned what he thought he knew. All his knowledge of America's original inhabitants was from westerns at the cinema showing 'Red Indians' and tepees, but *Mesa Verde* was a settlement of shallow caves and adobe constructions (houses, towers, pit houses, and religious meeting places) all built into the overhang of a canyon wall. Most amazing of all was 'Cliff Palace'.

'Native Americans who'd already been in this area for at least five hundred years, moved down into these cliff houses at about the time Becket was getting himself killed in Canterbury cathedral,' Helena said.

Steve thought he saw her eyes were wet, as she made this observation. Knowing that she always resisted sentimentality, he remembered that the only other time he'd seen her cry was when she was watching the scenes from Orgreave on TV. But, as they walked among the remains of the Puebloan houses, she'd been very touched, perhaps because it seemed to her as much as to him as if the original inhabitants had only recently left, their way of life abandoned overnight, no permanence to anything.

Maybe it was to assert herself that, after having related the Mesa Verde's inhabitants to the time of Becket, she immediately targeted President Reagan who, Steve had noticed, even as soon as she met him at Denver airport and drove him to Lost Angel Canyon, had become the stand-in for Mrs Thatcher.

Turning to look back for a last time at the cliff dwellings as they made their way to the car, she declared, 'Reagan quotes Tom Paine to justify his claim that America can begin the world over again and be anything it wants to be. I've a lot of time for Tom Paine, but what Reagan uses him for in this case is nonsense. Look at what we've just seen. This continent has a past, like everywhere else, and the past always overshadows the present. Terrible things were done to native Americans, not to speak of what happened to African slaves.'

If the past always overshadows the present, he wondered, where does that leave me, Portway and the O'Kanes?

But he was helped to ignore this question by enjoying seeing President Reagan on television nearly every night and hearing commentators say, 'He's making the nation feel good about itself again.' On his ranch the president wore jeans and a Stetson and road a horse as if he was in a cowboy film.

'He thinks he's still in the movies,' Helena commented, reminding Steve of Jan Woodhouse.

'The bullets that hit him in the assassination attempt were real enough,' Steve responded, causing her to give him a wary glance.

How would she behave politically in America, where, like him, she would have the status of an 'alien'? As he should have expected, she'd quickly informed herself, so as to have something to say, telling him that when George Bush, the vice-president, was running against Reagan for the nomination as Republican presidential candidate, he'd described Reagan's economic policy as 'Voodoo economics.'

'But now,' she asserted, 'he's entirely signed up to the policy and denying he ever used the term, "voodoo economics". What it amounts to is ultra-Thatcherism: anti-unions and social welfare, cut taxes for the rich, increase military spending. Meanwhile the nation's wealth is supposed to "trickle down" to the poor, who are required to be like Oliver Twist, holding out a dish to catch the drops and always knowing they should never ask for more. You wouldn't think Reagan's own father and brother were found jobs by Roosevelt's New Deal.'

Yet academics Steve had met, some with places in California or Florida, seemed to have caught plenty of drops, as did RMU itself two thousand feet below the mining cabin; its tree filled green campus expensively watered to prevent it returning to desert. Leisure time could be spent skiing, hiking, hunting, four-wheel driving in the mighty Rockies, while RMU's sports centre boasted facilities Canterbury could only dream of, including an Olympic-size pool supplying its customers with costumes and towels as part of their contract. For nearly every sport coaches advertised their services, revealing to Steve that Americans rarely did anything in an amateur way. To play tennis well (and why not?), they paid for lessons. He watched a women's soccer team practise and knew immediately he could improve its defence. But to be a soccer coach out here, he'd have to be qualified. To be anything in the States, he'd need qualifications, a problem that would take time to solve.

He never asked about Tom Paine, because he wanted to enjoy himself, and he drifted off whenever Helena unravelled again the wrongs American had committed to become America. If she wanted to prove she was coming over here without illusions, he could feel that he himself didn't have that many. Colorado, after all, wasn't completely different even from Atherstone. On this final night in Lost Angel Canyon before the flight back to England he was in bed with Helena near an abandoned mine, and there'd been abandoned mines thirty minutes walk from his and Gordon's bedroom in the family's first house. He remembered their names: *Nelson, Wellington, Pretoria*. When he was a kid people were still talking about a disaster at the *Pretoria* in the thirties with many miners killed. As a seven year old in the forties, when everything was rationed, Gordon had picked scraps of coal with his dad from the slag-heap of a nearby pit which was then still working, but which was closed down twenty-five years before the current miners' strike.

'Dad got hold of two motor-bike wheels and built a truck,' Gordon used to say. 'He stood between the shafts with a strap across his chest, like a horse. Up the hills, when the truck was loaded, I pushed at the back, bent-double like in illustrations of exploited child labour.'

What you had to do when you had next to no money.

XIV

Back in Canterbury, as soon as he'd recovered from jet lag, Steve talked to Mike Connery about his resignation.

'I know you can quit after a month's notice,' Mike said. 'But we need you to run the sports centre till the new assistant director finds her feet, and while we're searching for your replacement. You're just as much of a loss to us as Helena is,' he added anxiously, 'and she's a hell of a loss.'

So Steve agreed to stay on week by week, maybe till the end of October, knowing he would actually need some extra time to get his visa sorted. Helena would leave for Colorado by the last week of August, meaning they might be apart for two months or so.

For her final weekend in England he borrowed Yatsey's Luton to ferry her stuff to Oxford. The Thursday before, she took Jan Woodhouse and Steve to Canterbury's best French restaurant for a farewell dinner. Yatesy and Carol had been invited too, but Carol, in the last weeks of pregnancy, wasn't feeling up to it. The dinner was serenaded by Jan's wheezing chest and hacking cough.

'You're giving up Britain, and I'm giving up smoking,' she said to Helena. 'Look!'

She produced a dummy plastic cigarette in a holder tapering into a mouthpiece. Turning to Steve she said, 'What can the sports centre do to bring me back to health? And please, no jokes, either of you.'

'Steve never jokes about keeping fit,' Helena said. 'Anyway, as a parting gift, he's just appointed the kind of person you might be looking for.'

'It's the new assistant director,' he said, 'Gill Andrews. She's especially in charge of programmes for women. She can give you a personal assessment and recommend exercise routines for you.'

'I'll be there as soon as I've bought some tracksuits,' Jan said. 'I need to get my lungs fit for visiting you at altitude.'

In Oxford Helena's father greeted them in his drive, impressed by Steve's skill in reversing the Luton through his narrow gateway.

'I'm so disappointed not to see your sports car,' he said to Steve, shaking his hand warmly, and then hugging and kissing Helena. 'I've heard so much about it.'

Wearing comfortable corduroys, a V necked sweater and open necked shirt, he was welcoming them for what would be just a one night's stay. The next day, Sunday, was Helena's mother's birthday, when Helena always tried to visit her mother's grave. In the evening she was flying from Heathrow back to Denver.

'I'm afraid Helena's only been used to fairly ordinary estate cars,' Peter continued in the hall, 'and nowadays I've abandoned driving altogether, though Charles Furlow, my best friend whom you met in London, has one of the big Jaguar saloons, a Sovereign, I think.'

'Not having a car makes sense,' Steve said. 'Saves a lot of money.'

'Now you're being perverse,' Helena said to him. To her father she said, 'Steve walks everywhere, but every time he drives his car he falls in love with it all over again. And it is a thrill, all that leather and mighty energy. Even though the car's fairly new, it seems to belong to a period when people "motored". I sometimes think we should both be wearing those tight fitting leather hats with goggles, and sheepskin jackets, like pilots in films of the last war. I'll miss it.'

'Not as much as Steve, I'll bet,' Peter said.

When the Luton had been unloaded, and they were settled in, Peter said he would take them out for dinner, but Helena suggested they all eat in a more relaxed manner in the house.

'Of the three of us Steve's the only cook, so why don't he and I go and buy something for him to put together.'

With Peter's money they bought steaks, salads, French bread, and cheese.

'I want my father to see all your talents,' Helena said.

'I could do with some cream and olive oil.'

'You'd better buy them. They won't be in my father's kitchen.'

Back at the house Peter produced what he called 'A touch of Italy,' two wonderful bottles of Barolo. Then, drink in hand, he watched fascinated as Steve stood over his cooker, first sealing the meat in oil, before cooking it and placing it to one side 'to rest.' Next he did mushrooms and onions, finally deglazing the pan with red wine and cream. Telling Helena to 'be quick and finish the salad,' he poured the sauce over the meat.

'I've never tasted a better steak,' Peter said to Steve, pushing the second bottle in his direction and sitting back from his plate. 'I can see why Helena looks so wonderfully healthy, if you feed her like this. Her mother, my wife, was a dedicated cook, but I hardly cook at all. I take most of my meals in college.'

'There's the exercise, as well as the food,' Helena said. 'Steve's a perfect complement to my academic life.'

'I can see I've not paid enough attention to the physical side of things,' Peter responded resignedly. 'I walk to college, but it's no distance.'

Steve couldn't see him changing his habits at this stage in his life. Apart from walking to work, his main exercise would be moving his books about. Steve had never seen so many in a house, and they were already oppressing him, as if they were accusing him of everything he didn't know. Before they could eat, they had to clear them from the dining tablet, and they covered nearly every other surface and some parts of the floor. Even the downstairs loo was lined with what looked like a complete set of *Wisden*. How much did Helena's father need to know? Was his own dad so nearly helpless in his life, because he knew next to nothing? He was Labour, like Helena, but hardly belonged to the same world.

'He likes you, you know,' Helena said, when they were in bed together, he on his back, she on her front. 'I think he sees in your physicality and ability to engage with the world everything he's given up on. It's amazing, but I don't think he could actually go and choose food in a shop - other than basic things at any rate. He meets young and fit students, of course, but none like you. The only other man I've really brought back in the past was very different.'

'I suppose "really" means sleeping with you in this bed.'

'What does that matter? We've both had previous relationships.'

'I know,' he said.

Turning towards her, he ran his hand over her naked body - the wonderfully smooth slide down her back and up over her buttocks, 'How about a relationship now?'

'I was just about to make an offer,' she said softly, also turning towards him.

She woke him early in the morning for the walk to her mother's grave.

'You once told me your mother was an English teacher, like you,' he said.

'Yes, a school teacher. I have all her books. I love reading her comments in the margins. Sometimes I turn immediately to photographs of her and imagine this bright-eyed young woman speaking what I read. I have her hair, though mine's straight. I can see she had so much promise. Motor neurone disease cheated her - loaded gun, loaded dice.'

'Didn't your dad ever want to re-marry?'

'I don't think he wanted to risk ever being so hurt again. I noticed women around from time to time, but as I got older I saw he was burying himself in his work with the occasional relief of playing the piano. Perhaps the women also saw this recessiveness. Academics of his generation had no problem retreating into their work, especially in an Oxford college.'

From her shoulder bag she gave him a black and white photo in a special folder. It showed a young man, clearly Helena's father, and a young woman, also looking like Helena. Steve had seen several photos of this woman in the house, and he knew they were of Helena's mother, because he'd seen similar ones in Helena's flat in Canterbury. In the photo Helena produced the young couple (younger than Helena and Steve were now) were sitting smiling and relaxed, side by side in armchairs, apparently listening to someone talking to them.

'You can see how happy and in love they were,' Helena said after he returned the photo. 'They look so delighted to be in each other's presence, and it must have been a special joy for my father after his grief over his brother's death. He and my mother met as students at Oxford in their very first week. I don't think either had ever slept with another lover. My mother was forty-four when she died, not all that many years from where I am now. They'd been establishing their careers and had me a bit late.'

At the cemetery in the morning sunshine, he read on the rounded headstone:

LAURA MARGARET EDWARDS 1924-1968
Beloved Daughter Wife and Mother
What will survive of us is love

'The quotation's from a Larkin poem,' Helena said, sighing. 'It's a hope. I'm sure my father brings as many qualifications to it as Larkin himself did. He's not a historian for nothing. Reading Larkin's reviews in the *Telegraph* attracted my father to jazz. He actually met Larkin at a jazz concert.'

She'd bought three roses, which she laid before the headstone on the mown grass.

'One from my father, you, and me. My father will be coming later.'

Over a coffee in the city centre she said, 'My mother's first degree was just as good as my father's, but she never got anywhere in trying to start a university career. My father told me she was asked at two interviews for university jobs if she planned to have children. It wouldn't happen nowadays.'

'A victory for feminism.'

She was silent for a moment before saying, 'Feminism's not without problems. Powerful voices at Greenham Common are arguing heterosexuality's a sell-out. They claim men are redundant. There's pressure on women to become lesbians.'

'There's no way you're a lesbian.' Then, risking it, 'My sister's a kind of feminist.'

'Your sister! How?'

'Well she won't be bossed by any man for a start. I told you her husband's a miner, but she didn't let him go to Orgreave. She said he wasn't going to get his head bashed in so Arthur Scargill could be on television every night.'

Helena didn't reply. Orgreave had left her not knowing which way to turn.

'If anything my sister would like to be like Mrs Thatcher. She sees her as an example. She's passed every nursing exam in sight, and now with her kids in secondary school she's going back to college and learning about management. She thinks she might run a hospital some day.'

'Good luck to her. Even Jan, you know, sometimes finds herself defending Mrs Thatcher.'

'No!'

'What else can she do? She overhears miners saying brutish, sexual things about the prime minister, just because she's a woman; appalling things they'd like to do to her - ram into her.'

He didn't know how to answer this, so he said, 'Jan probably thinks I'm like these men. She doesn't seem to think I'm enlightened at all.'

'Oh, you'd be surprised how interested Jan is in you.'

Gulping his coffee in response, he then asked, 'Is Jan as troubled as you about the Labour party?'

He knew Helena didn't know how to respond as Labour broke apart over the miners and the rise of Militant in Liverpool and other cities. Why was he more impressed than she was by Militant Labour MPs who said they were living on the same wage as the average skilled worker? Wasn't that what Socialism was supposed to be about - equality?

All she said as she pushed her cup to one side was, 'As things stand now, I'm politically at a dead end. I'm settling in America where Mrs Thatcher's in bed with Reagan. I'm glad I've got this job, but I have to recognise universities the world over are nothing like what they were when my father began. They used to be a source of values. Now they're like stalls in a market place.'

Later that day they drove to Heathrow, where they hugged and kissed passionately as they parted. Then he was back in Canterbury for his final stretch at the sports centre, feeling full of exhilaration from what lay before him, and from how much he was now part of Helena's life. Passing the heavy bag hanging for the boxers, he smashed his fist into it, hurting his knuckles on its canvas. In the main hall, where an aerobics session was pounding full-on to Bonnie Tyler's 'I Need a Hero', he jumped on the platform alongside the leader, did some moves, then jumped off, arms outstretched, like Superman.

XV

It was Beatrice Furlow's first appearance on *Late Hour*, mingling with the 'culture tossers,' as the editor of the Sunday tabloid she starred in put it. *In Their Shoes* and her new show *Perky Thirty* had viewers in their millions, but she was confident that all they required from her was to offer her mainly women guests a series of unchallenging remarks leading to a stream of personal revelations. *Late Hour* might need her to have something like ideas, and she wasn't sure she had any. Operating very successfully in the world as she found it, she hadn't needed them. She simply followed her instinct for what she was sure everybody wanted to hear, and usually she was right.

She was diverted from her nervousness about appearing on the programme when she discovered that Jan Woodhouse from Canterbury University would also be on the show with her. From her father she'd learned several weeks ago that Helena Edwards was working at Canterbury as a lecturer and had met a man there in the sports department. So when she was introduced to Jan Woodhouse in the studio, before *Late Hour* was ready to be recorded, it was only natural she should mention Helena Edwards and she had been at school together, and then ask, 'Do you know her?'

'Yes, we're good friends.'

'I heard she had a new man who works in sports.'

'Steve Wilson - they're going to the States together.'

'Holiday, at this time of year, September; aren't they working!'

'No, it's nothing to do with a holiday. Helena's got a new job in Colorado. She's over there now. Steve will join her as soon as the university at Canterbury has found someone else to run the sports centre. Helena's job in Canterbury was only for one year, and her contract wasn't renewed. Financial problems in the English department, or so the university claimed.'

'Will Helena's man have a sports job in the States?'

'That depends. He doesn't have much in the way of qualifications for a job over there. Before arriving in Canterbury, where he's been a great success, he played football and then went into the army.'

'So what will he do?'

'He'll live with Helena, perhaps become a student. They love being together, simple as that. It's a good relationship, even though they often have completely different views on things, especially politically.'

Beatrice's researcher had told her Jan Woodhouse was a feminist firebrand, so she was surprised to find her so calm and older sisterly with respect to Helena and her man, and also so feminine in her clothes - soft ankle boots, purple tights, long silvery-grey paisley skirt, cream silk blouse, and a slightly darker, finely worked waistcoat she'd crocheted herself. It made Beatrice think she hadn't given enough thought to her own navy blue jacket and skirt, one of a dozen or so similar business outfits in her wardrobe, especially as she was covering the fashion item on *Late Hour*.

But, when it came to it, she was more than satisfied with her performance, for what didn't she know about fashion? It followed the film item led by Lionel Bailey, a self-styled 'Critic of the Contemporary', and again she held her own. Then it was current affairs and inevitably the miners.

Surprisingly, Fiona Brody, the presenter, turned first to her. What would she say? Only as she was beginning to speak did she remember that the material her researcher had found for her was actually from an article, two months old, by Jan Woodhouse herself. She was confident she'd memorised the argument and that it would please Jan Woodhouse. It was about the miners' wives.

'The achievement of these women is the only good to come out of the whole sorry mess,' she insisted. 'They are showing everybody, especially their husbands, what all women are capable of. They will never go back to their domestic rut. They are true revolutionaries, breaking free from dead patriarchal traditions.'

'Absolutely,' said Lionel.

'More or less rubbish, I'm afraid,' Jan Woodhouse responded calmly. 'I made the argument against this kind of sentimentality weeks ago. After the events at Orgreave in June I'm surprised it's still raising its head. What's revolutionary about working in a soup kitchen all day, feeding families as beaten down as your own? God knows I support women's equality and independence, but these women are being deluded and flattered by a gaggle of visiting London chatterers, like yourselves. They'll always be stuck with miserable jobs to make ends meet and requiring them to be as submissive as it's intended the miners must be. Working-class women are being used to break the unions their husbands belong to.'

Fiona Brody, 'another piece of BBC intellectual Edinburgh totty,' according to Beatrice's editor (from Stoke-on-Trent), decided to end the programme soon afterwards.

'I need a coffee,' Jan Woodhouse said as soon as the recording finished.

Beatrice followed her.

'Why attack me like that?' she challenged Jan, who was looking for somewhere to sit with her coffee.

'I wasn't attacking you. I was saying you were wrong.'

'You don't think I'm a serious person.'

'Why do you say that? I don't know you at all. We only met three hours ago.'

'Helena Edwards is a serious person.'

'Are you asking me or telling me? Either way, I'd say yes, she is.'

'Remember me to her.'

From the studio Beatrice shared a taxi with Lionel.

'Old bag,' he said of Jan Woodhouse, though he was only about five years younger. 'She should be kept off TV. Who wants to look at her? All that IRA Marxist shit she writes, all on taxpayers' money. The edit better make me and you look good, or I'll have somebody's balls! Why can't the Jan Woodhouses ever get real? Me and you, Beatrice, we ply our trade in the marketplace, where it has to be real. We earn! We're ready for the risky move, ready to stand or fall, ready for the twenty-first century.'

Quietening down he kissed her cheek, following this by placing the palm of his hand on her thigh. She seized his wrist just as his hand was about to slide higher, inside her thigh.

'I'm not ready for that move, Lionel.'

'Pity,' he replied. 'But suit yourself. Call me whenever you want a good time. Anybody can see you need some release. I hear Simon's never out of his cell at Wes's, or that torture chamber in your basement.'

Simon greeted her in the hallway. He was wearing a white T-shirt and a light-green track-suit.

'I'm sure you were wonderful,' he smiled, kissing the cheek Lionel had kissed, but keeping his hands to himself.

She'd fallen for his soft Irish voice as soon as she met him. He seemed so un-threatening, so accommodating. Now she wondered if everything about him was anything more than a mask - but for what?

'How have you spent your time?' she said, pulling him closer as she moved the zip of his track-suit top up and down; 'apart from in the basement.'

In the basement was a complete gym, Lionel's 'torture chamber'.

'Not just that,' Simon answered, resisting and then moving away. 'I've been trying to get hold of Shane. I've phoned every number he's ever had.'

How Beatrice wished she could come home from her world to something normal with Simon. Shane Webb was another of his fantastical associates, like Clarence, the bullet-headed ex SAS man, who was his personal trainer. Always unnervingly silent, Clarence would sometimes laugh explosively when you least expected it, as if, at the bottom of everything, was some mad joke only apparent to himself. As for Shane Webb, he was the tiny guitarist from West Hartlepool with the damaged spine. She'd mentioned him to her father. Occasionally, she and Simon would be watching TV together when one of Simon's groups would come on, and Simon would break into strangely silent laughter.

'That guy playing his guitar as if he's jerking off - he might as well be. He couldn't do that solo if he practised till he died. He's miming to what Shane laid down in the studio.'

'Is Shane his real name?' she'd asked when she first heard of him.

'Too right, it is. His dad's ex-merchant-navy, mad on black American blues and Country and Western. He put a guitar into Shane's hands as soon as Shane could hold it. Shane says the guitar on his knees used to prevent him falling forward. His mother died having him. It must have been a terrible birth. A novice midwife couldn't get him out.'

Engineering deception was becoming Simon's passion. A month ago, when one of his young technicians moved into a TV production company to add laughter-tracks to comedy shows, he was jubilant.

'Shows on TV don't have to do much that's funny any more,' he declared to her. 'The laughs are in the can before they've written a joke. Immortal audiences on tape are forever splitting their sides.'

Provoked by her silence, he went on, 'Who knows how far we can go with stuff that's not funny getting laughs! Funerals, war scenes - give them a laughter track. What does anybody's death matter? There's always somebody to step into your shoes. Every night people sit in front of TV needing to laugh, but there's a shortage of material to put laughter-tracks to.'

Was he serious! Was she serious, exploiting photographs of celebrities, taken whenever, to illustrate a crisis she'd created for them?

'Even in solitary confinement,' the controller of her network asked her at a recent party, 'would you tune in to *In Their Shoes* or *Perky Thirty*? People are only watching these shows because they're too shagged out to live. All that saves them is the money they make.'

'These miners, you know,' her father said last week, holding a glass of Margaux to the light. 'All they want is real work and the preservation of their communities.'

He'd called with his friend Peter, Helena Edwards' father, wanting to show him his daughter's house in Connaught Square, knowing he could have his run of the wine cellar, since Simon would at most drink a glass of whatever bottle was left unfinished.

Beatrice didn't watch the actual transmission of her first appearance on *Late Hour*. All evening, however, she could hear Jan Woodhouse saying of Helena Edwards and her man, 'They love being together, simple as that.'

She'd no idea if Simon, or anyone else, ever loved being together with herself.

XVI

'Wake up! Out of bed! Come and look at this!' Theresa shook Liam.

'Whaa?'

'On TV, downstairs. *The Grand Hotel*, Brighton; Norman Tebbit's on a stretcher, half dead, crippled at least. We've nearly killed the British prime-minister and wiped out her entire cabinet.'

Unwashed, his beard unkempt, and wearing only the T-shirt and boxer shorts he slept in, Liam joined her downstairs and, noticing breakfast was nowhere in sight, made himself a pot of tea. Even in her excitement she again thought this unit's done for if we don't move on from him.

'So that must have been it,' Liam said, going close to the screen and squinting at it.

'That must have been it! What do you mean?'

'Let's watch. Then I'll tell you.'

He found his glasses, and they sat in front of the television, transfixed by its revelations: the jagged gash from top to bottom in the proud white front of the hotel, the emergency services clambering carefully over the rubble, the confirmation of five dead and many injured, the prime-minister herself only a few feet away from assassination.

Everything's moving our way, Theresa thought. Tebbit in his pyjamas on that stretcher, his face twisted in pain; the whole world can see British Government ministers aren't safe, even in their beds. We've destroyed their sleep forever.

But as the day developed, she began to focus in confused wonderment on the prime minister, the woman who should now have been dead.

She saw and heard the prime minister proclaim, 'It was an attempt to cripple Her Majesty's democratically elected government'.

Suddenly Theresa realised that Mrs Thatcher had become the heroine in a drama the IRA had created for her. Like Britannia, Mrs Thatcher was showing she could never be broken - by the IRA, the miners, communists, enemies the world over.

Whose triumph is this Brighton bomb? Theresa asked herself. When is there ever a victory? Is Liam played-out because he knows he doesn't know?

Silencing Mrs Thatcher with the remote control, and needing to encourage herself, she announced suddenly, 'We must do something.'

'What? Do what?' Liam asked, bewildered.

At least he was now washed and dressed, after he'd made himself some toast. Slumped back in the chair, his legs were hanging sideways over the arm nearest to her.

'A follow-up,' she said.

'A follow-up? What, you mean to this bomb? You know we're not that kind of top team.'

'Not on this scale, our scale. It doesn't matter if it's small, as long as it spreads panic: "Where next? What next?" We can't be a sleeping cell forever.'

Getting no response, she added, 'Sean and Matthew need some action, and Pat's close to losing it. They could all get careless.'

'Look, we've already played our part,' Liam insisted. 'But for us this Brighton job could have been off.'

'What do you mean?'

'Captain Portway. He was fucking things up in Sussex, getting in the way. I was told to move him, bring him down here.'

'We were a decoy!'

'If you like, but important. Look what you've been watching since this morning.'

'And you knew!'

'Only that something big was planned. I didn't know what or where or when. I didn't even know it was going to be in Sussex, let alone Brighton. It could have been another London job. I was just told to make ourselves visible, take that captain away. Make sure he was on to us and following us.'

'I never could work out why we all suddenly moved the best part of a hundred miles. But what about Portway and the O'Kanes, when you came back from London with that photograph?'

'That was an unexpected bonus, "buy one get one free".'

All this information fired her up more. 'I just want to be nearer the centre of things,' she persisted.

'Give it time. You'll be there. You're good. You've crossed the line. You've killed in cold blood. McKnight's where you want him. I'm making sure the right people now about you.'

Then he said, 'But what's this about the others?'

But she didn't answer immediately. She didn't like her future depending on him.

'Sean and Matthew are men too, you know,' she said, after several minutes. 'They can't do without women, and they're sick of travelling about for whores. They're shagging local tarts near their place in Dover. It's risky, dangerous.' Letting this sink in, she added, 'Matthew said to me the other day you have it made, a forty- year- old living with a twenty-two- year old; but he supposed that was the commander's privilege.'

'Forty-year-old! Fuck him! What did you say?'

'That you could control yourself because you trained to be a priest. But Matthew had his answer ready. He told me you must need women, or you'd have completed the training and taken the boys.'

'He'd better watch his mouth. He's looking at a knee-capping.'

'That's a waste. Use him for something positive. Bring us all together again. Stop Pat drifting away.'

While Liam stroked his beard and considered this, she cajoled, 'I can see we've played a part in something big, but can't we now do something for ourselves, something random here in a wide-open place like Kent, where nobody's expecting anything?' Catching his eye, she pressed him, 'Use your influence. Get clearance for an operation. We can't recce targets forever. We've earned a reward.' Pausing, she added in a softer voice, 'I always reward you.'

His hand left his beard and reached towards her.

'I know that, my little jockey, my Saint Theresa,' he conceded. 'Come over here.'

She sat on the floor at his feet, while the hand that had been stroking his beard, ran its fingers through her hair.

'I'll go up to London, talk to people,' he murmured.

'Be forceful,' she urged, her voice still soft, her eyes seeing Mrs Thatcher mouthing on the silent screen.

XVII

Everything was fixed up for Steve's replacement at the sports centre, and he had his plane ticket to fly to Denver on the tenth of November, nearly a month away. But this sunny and crisp October Sunday afternoon he was waiting for Yatesy at Yates's Car Breakers And Repairers, which was now well on the way to being sold, so Yatesy's parents could retire to Spain.

Yatesy had phoned him during the week.

'If you've time on your hands on Sunday, come and help me put a rad in my Luton. My dad's got a Luton in the yard that's been smashed up from the back. Help me get the rad out and put it in mine.'

It had been arranged that for his last night in England Steve would drive over to Restore and cook Yatesy and Carol a parting meal before sleeping in their cottage. The next morning would be Steve's final drive in the Jag. With Yatesy he'd drive it to Heathrow. Yatesy would drive it back and sell it.

But he was happy to spend more time with his friend, helping him fix the Luton. There'd been a leak in its radiator, when he borrowed it to drive to Oxford and Heathrow with Helena and her stuff. He could still see Helena in the passenger seat on the way to the airport, excited, but also on edge, about her future. On the calendar in his kitchen he marked off every passing day before he would be joining her. He was like a prisoner in his cell waiting for release.

The Brighton bomb was just over a week ago, and Helena and he had discussed it in every phone call since: the scale of the IRA's ambition, whatever the security arrangements; the murderous violence.

'Oh, to have you over here!' Helena had said again last night.

But for now he would mark off another day helping Yatesy, telling himself again that no-one could know of their connection with Portway and the O'Kanes, because there had been no report, no record, of the handover of the O'Kanes to Portway. No records meant Portway's parents were getting nowhere. After the ambush had gone wrong in March eighty-one, all the authorities wanted to do was cover it up without acknowledging there'd even been an ambush. They sprayed British heroism all over it.

Waiting for Yatesy he walked up and down the aisles of wrecks, some of them resting on top of one another three and four cars high. He remembered coming to places like this when he was younger and had his first motor, a Vauxhall Viva. Because parts at a breaker's were miles cheaper than new parts, and because you learned to put them in your own car by taking them out of the wreck, you felt on top of things, ahead of the game. Today, though, more than ten years older, Portway and the O'Kanes on his mind, and what he would do personally with his life uncertain, he was less sure you could get ahead of anything. Some of these twisted and rusting wrecks weren't as old as his Jag. Any pleasure they'd provided had soon vanished. Screaming people had died inside them, their bodies ripped apart or burned alive in every day motorway wars. He thought of Alex Graham at United. After the drunken crash in Glasgow it leaked out there'd hardly been enough left of Alex to arrange in a coffin.

He was back at the entrance to the breakers just as Yatesy arrived in the Luton, greeny-brown water spurting from the radiator grill.

Steve was in an old bomber-jacket, but climbing into the cab he noticed Yatesy was only in a T shirt, his shoulder and chest muscles bulging through it, as if he generated his own energy.

'You haven't started then?' Yatsey said to him.

'I'm out of practice. Jaguar owners don't get involved in this kind of stuff.'

'Jaguar owners! I hope you've put that car of yours somewhere safe. My dad's likely to sell a bit off it.'

'He let me park it with his Mercedes and the Alsatians. He had to drive the dogs back before I could open my car door.'

'Bloody good dogs. Would you fancy trying to nick anything from the yard at night once they've been roused? But have you seen my dad wrestle with them? They're like playful pups.'

They drove a short distance down a lane of wrecks to the smashed Luton, Yatesy parking bonnet to bonnet, with a couple of yards in between.

'Bringing my van down here's a special privilege. I'm the owner's son,' he announced to a man who looked up in surprise from the rear hub of a Volvo.

'This'll be done in no time,' he then said to Steve. 'You do as much as you can taking the rad out of my van, while I tackle the other. I might need you again before you go to America, to help with the gearbox. That in my van's as good as knackered. It makes this droning noise, like there's a shit-scared ghost in the cab. We could make the business pay for a new van, but I don't want too much debt.'

'Carol OK?' Steve asked, as he began to sort out the tools he needed.

'Yup, pregnancy's still going well. The help we employ for the business gives her plenty of time to rest and make sure the books are straight. Looking at things all round, we couldn't be doing better. The scaffolding's gone up to extend the cottage. Another bloke we were at school with.'

'Who weren't you at school with!'

'You know, we all failed the Eleven Plus, but some of us have done OK. This lad went into his dad's scaffolding business. For his special customers he has these cards.'

He took out a card from his back pocket. It read:

Randy Towers
Scaffolding
Best Erection in Town

Steve laughed. 'Carol seen it?'

'I showed it her straight away. Randolph didn't half fancy her at secondary school. I think she might have been the love of his life, even at fifteen, and if it hadn't been me, he might have been her bloke.'

As they both began draining the rads Steve thought he could see Yatsey re-imagining his early love life.

'Anyway,' Yatsey went on, coming back to the present, 'Randolph took a lot of stick till he was about fourteen or fifteen because of his name. I mean, nobody was called Randolph, and as for "Randy" at the secondary modern! Then he suddenly shot up, really lived up to his last name - six foot odd and a very fast bowler. Lads didn't bully him any more, because of his height, but mainly because they knew he could smash their nuts with a cricket ball, box or no box. The games teacher used to make any real bastards bat against him, hoping they'd piss in their pants. He wanted him to have a trial for the county, but Randolph said there was more money in scaffolding. He's never had a permanent woman, though he likes them, and they've always liked him. On that score he's lived up to his first name on that card, plus he drives a Porsche. He's like you. He's always known the car he wanted.'

So many mates even from school, Steve thought. Why did I never have them?

They'd been working for about forty-five minutes and nearly had both radiators out. Suddenly a young man was standing between the vans. He was tall, with long blond hair and John Lennon glasses.

'I wonder if you can lend me a spanner,' he said.

'What's it for?' Yatesy asked.

'I'm trying to get the back bumper off a VW Beetle. This spanner's no use. It fits the nuts but it won't turn them.'

He showed them what must have been a tool for his bike, a flat, short piece of metal with holes and notches in it.

'Bugger me, I could turn nuts better with my fingers,' Yatesy said. 'Come on, Stevey, we can have a quick look. Bring my socket set.'

They walked about thirty yards to the Beetle, Steve carrying the socket set.

'Yeah, the nuts are rusted, but my socket set should do it,' Yatesy said. 'I better get it off for you. It won't take a minute.'

He selected one of the sockets from the tray and then took out the ratchet lever. In about fifteen minutes the bumper was in the lad's hands.

'That's great, fantastic,' he said, hardly believing he was actually holding it.

'You should buy one of these,' Yatesy said, putting the pieces of the socket set back into the tray. 'Though from what I know about Beetles this tool set'll be too heavy for your car to carry.'

The lad smiled. 'There's just me and my girlfriend,' he said.

'I bet there is. You're a student, right?'

'Yeah, English, at the university.'

'Did you know a teacher called Helena?' Yatesy asked.

' Dr Edwards? Yeah, she's left. It's a pity. She was great. Made us laugh and worked us hard.'

'Yeah, well she's a friend of ours.'

Offering his hand to Yatesy the student said, 'I can't thank you enough.' To Steve he nodded, then said, 'Don't you work in the sports centre at the university? I play in the five-a-side league you started.'

'You could say he works in the sports centre,' Yatesy said, laughing.

As they walked back to the Lutons, Steve said, 'Most people have no bleeding idea of the hassle I've been through this last twelve months.' He was suddenly glad to be getting shot of everything to do with the sports centre. It was why he hadn't responded to the student.

But all Yatesy said, as they reached the Lutons, was, 'Dr Edwards, eh! I wouldn't mind being under a doctor like that.'

'Oh yeah!'

'No, you know I don't mean anything, Stevey.' He wiped his hands on a rag. 'It's bloody difficult, you know, with Carol being pregnant. She doesn't want any messing around. She's worried about harming the baby. I bought a *Playboy* last week, first time since I came out of the army. Didn't do me much good. It's in the van under the seat.' Then, after another pause, he looked Steve in the eyes. 'I wouldn't think of playing away. I wouldn't break what me and Carol have.' Again he paused before saying, 'She's what I know about love, Stevey - going to sleep with her, wakening up with her, I can face any day.'

'You're a lucky man,' Steve said, calm again. 'I liked Carol the first time I met her. Apart from looking great, she just gets on with things. She doesn't create problems, where there aren't any.'

'It's down to you we're together at all. I'll never forget it. Neither will Carol.'

'What do you mean?'

'When you saved my life.'

Now it was Steve's turn to pause, before he said, 'That was just in a battle. You'd have done the same for me. And I do want to forget it, but it's always stayed with me.'

Immediately it flashed back into his mind: taking an Argy position, basic killing with bayonets; an Argy coming from behind at Yatesy, him coming from behind at the Argy; thrusting his bayonet up through the Argy's right side and under his ribs; the dying face twisting round at him, as he dumped the small body onto the ground and put his foot on it to yank out the bayonet.

'You ...,' it cursed, with its last breath.

Breaking the silence, Yatesy said, 'You're not out of your league with Helena, you know, even though she's special, especially when she gets talking.'

'Thanks,' he replied, smiling and forcing himself back into the scene at the breaker's yard.

By now all that was left to do was for Yatesy to put the replacement rad into his van, Steve holding and passing over tools. Looking back up the yard where there were areas covered and uncovered for servicing, he could see a man working on a fairly old Maestro, and another man attending to the back light of a Cortina. Part of Yatesy's dad's business was repairs for people who couldn't afford regular garages - low-paid workers, pensioners, single mothers, all struggling to keep a car on the road, and put it through its MOT.

'Notes, o'course,' Steve had heard Yatesy's dad say when he named a price. Cash, with no invoices or receipts, kept the price low.

'When he's finished a job, even with second-hand parts, my dad sometimes has to charge more than the car's worth,' Yatesy had told him. 'But nobody'll do it cheaper. Pensioners (husbands and wives) will come together, though the wife doesn't drive and knows nothing about cars. You can see them reckoning up the pounds when they're given a price that's near to a whole week's pension for them both. You wonder what they're sacrificing, so they can keep a car on the road the manufacturer doesn't even want to remember. The wife knows how much it means to him to have a car. He knows she likes to be driven to do the shopping and visit the grandchildren and her sisters. Well, it gives my dad a living.'

Whatever the politics people want their own lives, Steve thought, sure that Helena would immediately come back at him, if she was here and he said it to her. He'd have to get used to always being challenged, especially when he was dependant on her.

'Job done,' Yatsey groaned now, straightening up and massaging his back. 'Let's have a coffee in the office, and then I'll come back and fill up the new radiator. I'll get that *Playboy*. I've promised it to one of the lads.'

In the grimy, cluttered shed that passed as an office Steve drank the brown liquid Yatesy handed to him. Nothing it says on the jar makes this coffee, he thought.

Then, looking through the window, he saw a slight, very pretty young woman, with hair as black as his own. She was standing by the Cortina with notes in her hand, obviously wanting to pay for the repair. It was the woman Helena and he had bumped into on the Churches Walk, when that bloke with the ginger hair who was with her sprained his ankle, the woman who'd been in the cathedral months ago, when Helena was telling him about Becket. Also looking through the window Yatesy saw her too and went out to collect her money.

'Very tasty,' he said, referring to the woman, when he came back into the office with the notes in his hand. He'd opened the door of the Cortina for her and helped her untangle the seat belt.

'That's why you gave her valet service,' Steve answered, thinking how strange it was that he kept coming across this woman. She'd catch any man's eye, for sure.

XVIII

Even before the phone was to his ear, Carol's broken voice was already sobbing, 'Steve, Joe's car's exploded. Police are here. He's dead!'

Hands clenched into his hair after he put the phone down, Steve exclaimed in torment, 'Jesus Christ, I was with him sixteen hours ago!'

'Portway, O'Kanes, O'Kanes Portway' pounded through his skull, as he drove through morning commuters having their normal day.

On Nackington Road two police cars, sirens blaring and flashing, hurtled past him.

He'd saved Yatesy's life so the IRA could kill him.

When he reached Restore, it was already becoming a crime scene, readying itself for the media assault. White screens were being erected to shield the area around the tiny wrecked Nissan Yatesy used daily to drive to and from jobs. It stood on blackened concrete alongside the damaged Luton and the damaged barn. Glimpsing Yatesy's huge upper body, his shoulder and head slumped diagonally against the window of the passenger door, Steve remembered his friend joking about the Nissan, 'I'm buying a bigger pram for the baby!' Soon he would learn there was hardly anything left of Yatesy's lower body. He was bleeding to death before the ambulance left its base.

Explaining he was Joe Yates's best friend, and Carol had phoned him, Steve was allowed to go to the cottage. Under the vertical and horizontal tubes of Towers Scaffolding, it looked like a fortress. The *Macbeth* with its scaffolding platforms he'd seen with Helena flashed into Steve's head. Now, as in a TV play, a police man and a police woman were guarding the cottage door, while chatting casually and occasionally skipping from foot to foot to keep warm.

Inside Yatesy's parent, Bill and Annie, sat together on a sofa, Annie crying silently. Carol's mother and oldest sister were upstairs with a nurse, looking after Carol whose baby was already overdue. Carol had gone to the Nissan in her dressing gown after hearing the explosion. She'd dialled 999. Bill Yates had confirmed to the police it was his son in the car. Already he was trying to transform grief into anger.

'IRA, Stevey!' he challenged as Steve entered. 'You better watch it. The bastards are going for unarmed ex-soldiers.'

'What happened? Are we sure it's not an accident?'

'Fucking accident!' His wife looked a rebuke at him. 'No chance. No car blows up like that on its own. This is a follow-up to Brighton. By Christ, if we could ever get hold of who did this, I know people who'd make 'em scream like pigs.' Then, to his wife as sobs broke his voice, 'They've murdered Joe! That's two sons we've lost!'

Like everyone else, Steve learned the device in the Nissan exploded as soon as Yatesy switched on the ignition. Straight after breakfast he was off to work. He came out of the cottage, opened the big gates onto the road, sat in the car, turned the key, and was blown in half. As the media were soon to script it, 'evil cowards' had murdered a random ex-soldier because of his service in Northern Ireland, and 'a new born baby boy would now have no daddy.' In the peaceful Kent countryside during the night, it had been all too easy for 'these monsters' to fix an explosive device under the car of the unsuspecting Joe Yates, and 'we can only be glad Carol Yates's car, parked in front of the cottage, was not chosen, or we might have been reporting the death of a heavily pregnant woman and her unborn child!'

No mention anywhere of Portway and the O'Kanes, leaving Steve to wonder if killing Yatesy really was random, and he himself was in no more danger than any other ex-squaddie. For Christ's sake, he had to consider himself, even as Yatesy lay blown apart! Oh to be with Helena in Colorado! Escape everything! Why had all this happened in his life?

Phoning Helena he used a call box, in case his house phone was bugged. At first she could hardly speak from shock and crying. When he phoned her the next night, he could also say Carol had safely had a baby boy.

'What a father to miss,' she half sobbed. 'Joe was so honourable and strong and kind. I thought Carol and he were so easy with each other, full of love and respect for each other.'

Then she was crying again, till she recovered and said, still with tears in her voice, 'As I talk about them, it's as if Joe's still alive. It's all so unreal for me over here, but it must be oh so real for you, and I worry about you so much. Suppose the killing was connected with that Captain Portway. Oh, I so want you over here and safe.'

Military and anti-terrorists interviewers grilled him, asking him if he knew any special reason Joe Yates was targeted.

Were they playing a game? They must know about Portway and the O'Kanes, so why not about him and Yatesy? Why was he not being warned, protected? Were they dangling him as bait? For fuck's sake Yatesy and him walked the O'Kanes no more than forty yards! Any other two unlucky bastards could have done it, except he was corporal, and he'd just sorted the men out when they were putting their fists and boots into the O'Kanes. That's why the sergeant picked him, and let him pick Yatesy, who needed cooling down - two ordinary soldiers, doing their time, earning their money, waiting for new lives to happen with nothing hanging over them.

He tried to fend off media interviews, but appeared in a local studio with Randolph Towers and the student Yatesy helped with the back bumper for the Beetle.

Randolph said Joe, 'Would never hurt anybody by word or deed; always ready to do anybody a good turn.' When he was a kid, Joe had stopped big lads from bullying him.

The student told what had happened in the scrap yard.

Steve said, 'All of it was just like Joe. In Northern Ireland and the Falklands there was nobody better, any rank, to have at your side.'

He had his plane ticket for the first of November, but he thought he better postpone his flight till after Yatesy's funeral, though nobody knew when the body would be released, making it impossible for Helena to re-arrange her teaching and fly back.

Assuming the media story was true, that Yatesy was killed by the IRA as a random ex-soldier, should he try to live normally: see to his final responsibilities at the sports hall, run with Mike Connery, or even alone - anything to exhaust himself so he could sleep? He was due to drive up and see his family and his dad, most likely for the last time. They were all stressed by any danger he might be in. Jan Woodhouse wanted to take him out for a meal, and the Connerys fed him a couple of times, saying he could stay with them if he postponed his flight. He visited Carol, hugging and kissing her, and gently kissing her baby son, who already looked like a ready-made replacement for Yatesy.

Yatesy! Yatesy! Yatesy! Never to be alive again! Ever! Impossible! All that mighty body gone! That nearly endless good nature.

'Gentle giant,' as the media truthfully said.

He straight away shouldered his way into that blazing clothes shop in Belfast. Women were screaming and frenzied outside the shop, when they passed on a routine patrol. The fire brigade was on its way, but a little girl was trapped in the basement. Fighting their way through the smoke and flames, Steve remembered following Yatesy without thinking how they were going to get back out. When they re-appeared with Yatesy holding the three- year-old, the mother and other women hugged and kissed them till they prised the women's arms from round their necks; uniforms nearly burnt off them both.

'Next thing, they'll be pissing and shitting on us again,' Yatesy said to him with a laugh on their way back to the base. Two days earlier there'd been a shooting, and they'd climbed down into the big sewer manholes looking for the weapon. Pipes discharging into the manholes were blocked with bungs during the search, but they still expected every Catholic in the neighbouring houses to be having a deliberate crap in the hope of flushing it on a British soldier.

Removing the bungs was the job of the newest recruit as he climbed out last.

Whoever he was, a grinning Yatesy always reached down to help the lad up onto the road.

XIX

Feel sorry and you were useless against a system that never felt sorry for you, Theresa insisted to herself. That woman's man had patrolled Ireland with a loaded gun in his hands, ready to put a bullet in any of her brothers, and in any Nationalist. Hundreds of crying women and fatherless children were down to men like him. She was proud to be their avenger.

Sunday lunchtime with Liam in a country pub near Ashford. The television mounted high on a wall was showing still photographs of Joe Yates; then, again, a photograph of Carol Yates sitting in a hospital bed and holding her new-born baby son. The same photos were in all the newspapers brought into the pub by Sunday regulars.

Liam was downing a pint at the bar. Roused by what the unit had achieved he'd been on top of her again as soon as he woke up.

Loathsome!

Everything was breaking in on her again, like when she was twelve, thirteen, fourteen.

She couldn't forget Joe Yates opening her car door for her.

'Seat belt,' he reminded her, untangling it from behind the driver's seat, their hands touching (his - big, rough, warm) as he handed her the metal tongue, so she could pull it across herself and click it in. 'Drive safe.'

Killing Portway was real, but like in a play, like she was playing a part. She knew nothing about his life and hardly saw his face until he was dead and not much then.

He was alive. He was dead. Take a bow, centre stage. Drop the curtain.

But for Joe Yates she wasn't centre stage any more, just a driver again, delivery woman, taking orders. She couldn't do explosives. That was down to Sean and Matthew.

Through the black unlit country roads she'd ferried them in the Land Rover, then waited a quarter of a mile away from the target. If anything went wrong, everybody was on their own, making a break for it in separate, rehearsed directions.

'No problem,' Sean said, climbing back into the Land Rover with Matthew, leaving her with no more to do than to take them to their house near Dover, where they burned all the clothes they'd worn and the rucksacks they'd used. When the device went off, they were on the way to their employment as casual labourers in one of O'Connor's road-laying gangs.

'We stay put, because nobody's on to us, and we might have another hit, here or somewhere else.' Liam said. 'There's more to that photograph.'

He meant the photograph he'd brought back from London showing Joe Yates as the new target. She'd seen most of it before: the O'Kanes with Portway on their left, taking them into custody. But now, on the O'Kanes' right, was Joe Yates, handing them over.

'And it must be another squaddie on the right of him,' Liam said. 'You can see the toe of his boot. He must be another target. Why not ours?'

But now he was harmonising with the regulars.

'IRA, scum of the earth.'

'Cut the army loose. Go in hard. Wipe them out, once and for all.'

'Wash our hands of the whole bloody lot. Leave them to it. Let them kill one another at their own expense.'

'Look at that poor woman.'

Here the whole bar going through its sentimental routine, gazing again at the still-shot on TV of the mother and baby.

Madonna and child.

Yesterday the anniversary of her abortion.

Men unzipping, women opening up; all the regulars having an orgy over Ireland; the media in a feeding frenzy.

Feeling faint and dizzy, she closed her eyes, gripping her half-pint glass tightly in both hands.

So much death: her baby, Captain Portway, Joe Yates, feet and legs blown away.

For what?

Men and women, all of them dying, never better than regulars.

Et expecto resurrectionem mortuorum.

'Even within the church, Theresa,' Sister O'Leary had told her, 'none of us can be good enough. But only the church can give us our lives. Outside the church you have only your death.'

'Are you all right?' It was Liam, back from the bar, leaning over her. 'You've hardly touched your shandy.'

Turning to several of the drinkers with an explanatory smile, almost a nod and a wink, he said, 'I think we should be getting back. She's not been a hundred per cent.'

He put a hand under her arm, and helped her to her feet. Once outside she recovered enough to say, 'I'm all right. Let me go.'

They walked slightly apart to the Cortina. She'd said nothing about the repair to the back light.

My true life, she was thinking. Where is it?

XX

Every day Steve checked under his car, even when he wasn't using it. He didn't know what he faced any more, whether he was coming or going.

'Oil leak,' he said to a neighbour.

Nearly two months since he'd touched Helena. No amount of pumping iron relieved his frustration. Her nearness on the phone made him desperate to clutch her, run his hands over her body, make love to her.

Soon his flight would take off for Denver, Colorado without him. He was here till after Yatesy's funeral, which couldn't be arranged till the body was released. Wanting a procession and a scene while outrage was high, the local council and the media were losing patience. Carol was keeping herself sane by devoting all her days to her baby, little Joey.

Steve left his house only in daylight. Outside his house he tried to make sure he was always visible. He had the local bus service (to and from the university campus, to and from town for food) timed to the minute. Never before in his life had he done so little walking to places. Before Yatesy's death he'd felt like a prisoner, marking off the days till he could fly to Helena in Colorado. Now he felt he was in solitary, with no-one to turn to for help.

'You're looking after yourself?' his brother Gordon had asked anxiously on the phone.

The call was mainly about their dad, Gordon wondering when Steve might pay their dad a visit.

'All the media seem to think the killing of your friend was random,' Gordon said.

Steve could sense his brother wanting to be encouraging at the same time as concerned. Gordon was the last person to take lightly the murder of Yatesy.

'I can't imagine what your friend's wife is going through with her new born son,' he continued.

Finally, as they were about to hang up, he said, 'Mum's worried about you, Stephen. We're all worried about you.'

'I'll come and see dad soon,' Steve responded, wondering, if the IRA really were after him, how he could risk bringing this danger to his family.

Then the name, Charles Furlow, was planted in his head during a phone call from Helena.

As always now, he'd taken the call from her lying on his back on the sofa. He'd given up using the call box at the corner of the street. What the hell, if someone was bugging his phone. Bring it on!

Helena and he had reminisced about the good times they'd had and looked forward to more. She'd mentioned the lunch in Covent Garden, before they both went to see *Macbeth* in the evening; how immediately her father had liked him.

'You know,' she said, 'I think he was even showing you off before his friend, Charles Furlow. You remember, Charles Furlow, who'd been in Kenya? We talked about his daughter, Beatrice. I was at school with her - the "Carmen Killing"?'

Still lying on the sofa and holding the phone on his chest after the call was over, he remembered that lunch vividly. Hadn't Helena's father hinted that Charles Furlow was in the secret services? It followed up what Helena herself had said when they did that walk to St Margaret's Bay and back last March. She'd more or less boasted about the father of her school friend being in MI5. He'd teased her about it.

Wouldn't Charles Furlow be able to find out if the killing of Yatesy had anything to do with the O'Kanes? If he could say it hadn't, Steve knew he'd have no more to worry about than any other ex-soldier who'd done tours in Northern Ireland. All the weight he'd been carrying would be lifted from him, like when Yatesy used to relieve him of a barbell he was struggling under, because he'd been too ambitious. Charles Furlow had been very friendly at the lunch, talking about commanding troops in Kenya. Surely he'd help. A soldier always backed another soldier.

He had Helena's father's phone number. As always Peter greeted him warmly.

'Hello, Stephen. What a welcome surprise. How are you?'

'I'm doing OK, Peter. Can't wait to join Helena.'

'It must be soon now, and she's told me she can't wait to see you.'

'Thanks. That's always good to hear, especially from you. In fact I've just spoken to Helena myself. She talked about that lunch in Covent Garden, when I first met you.'

'Ah yes, my friend Charles Furlow was there. You impressed him.'

'Glad to hear that. Actually, it's him I'm phoning you about.'

'Really? Why?'

'Peter, I might have a big problem, though it might not be a problem at all. I need someone to find out something for me, about when I was a soldier in Northern Ireland. I was wondering if your friend Charles Furlow could help.'

'How?'

'Isn't he in the secret services? Helena more or less said so to me once, and you ...'

'Ah, you remember my joke at the lunch. We used to keep very quiet about these things, but now Charles is on the verge of early retirement, he's hardly taking his job seriously himself.'

'Have you heard about the O'Kane brothers?' Steve asked. 'They've been in the news.'

'I've seen the photographs in the papers.'

'My friend Joe Yates, who was killed, and me - we were involved with them in Northern Ireland. I need to find out if the killing of my friend has anything to do with the O'Kanes. I thought Charles Furlow might help.'

'And you're phoning me because you want me to ask him.'

'Yes.'

'Well, it will break absolutely new ground in our long friendship. I've never asked anything like this of Charles before.' Then, when Steve said nothing, 'What does Helena know about all this?'

'She knows something about the O'Kanes and me. She doesn't know I'm phoning you.'

'Might you be in any kind of danger?'

'Yes, I might be.'

'Leave it with me.'

The next evening Peter returned the call.

'Steve, I didn't get far at all with Charles; nowhere in fact. Suddenly he was all seriousness about his work; more so than he's been for the last five or six years. He said the O'Kane business was strictly military. Nothing to do with him. Even if he tried, he wouldn't be able to get anywhere near it. He remembered you instantly, however. He asked me to give you his very best wishes.'

XXI

The next day, Friday, in the settling mist of the afternoon, Steve decided he'd jog from his house, twice around the campus perimeter road, and then back home. Risk, or no risk, he told himself. If I don't have a run, my legs will fall off.

He remembered a Yorkshire Para. 'Muck or nettles,' the Para used to say, 'Let's do it.'

On the campus he jogged past one of the new university security personnel on a walking patrol. Too fat to catch anybody in a chase, he thought. Like most of them.

Soon he was on his second lap of the perimeter road, which, on a Friday afternoon, was deserted. On the left, behind high hedges, were new student residence blocks already built on the university's first sports fields. The new sports facilities, reaching to farmland, a village church and an oast house, were to the right. Fifty yards ahead were the car park and the splendid new pavilion opened in his first month as director by a Kent cricket star. He saw a grey Land Rover in the car park, probably belonging to the Estates department, though he couldn't think why they'd be there at this time. Not my responsibility any more, he concluded. Another twenty minutes I'm home under the shower.

But as he reached the pavilion, two big men ran from behind it straight into his face, smashing him down onto his back onto the road, and nearly stunning him.

Jesus! This is it, he thought, as they grappled him face down onto the road, pushing his face into the tarmac, and as a third man pushed a pistol into the back of his head, boring it harder and harder, until he ceased struggling and was still.

Flattened on the road he heard a student come out from a nearby block behind the hedge and begin to empty bottles into a rubbish container.

'Some party,' she shouted to a friend.

'Get up,' the man with the gun said. 'We're walking to a Land Rover in the car park. You get in through the back door and lie face down on the floor with your head facing the windscreen. Think on. We can shoot you here and now and running will be the least of your problems.'

With the gun in the middle of his spine, they hustled him into the Land Rover, whose bench seats went lengthways. Hooding him they forced him down between the seats. Boots resting on the back of his head pressed his face into the floor, as the Land Rover started and drove off. Yeah, this is it, he thought again, surprised that he wasn't afraid, almost feeling relief that he had something definite to face, at last.

It seemed ages before the Land Rover crunched onto pebbles and stopped. Pulling him out of the Land Rover, they ran him stumbling into what must be a house, where they smacked him through an internal door, before manacling his hands and feet, the connecting chain pulling him into a bowed position, the thick hood keeping him in complete darkness.

'You won't need the time anymore,' one of the men said, removing his watch which must be still racing away the seconds for his run. 'Nice item, this.'

He was thrust onto a straight chair.

'Want to know why you're here,' the voice which had had the gun asked from behind him. 'I'm going to show you something from our people in London who are up the arses of your people in London. Don't turn round. The hood will be snatched off. I'll hold something for you to see. Then the hood's back on.'

Suddenly he was looking at a photograph: left to right - himself, Yatesy, the O'Kanes and Portway. He was just thinking how young

158

he and Yatesy looked, and noticing he was now in a farmhouse-type kitchen, when the hood was back on.

'You marched Paul and James O'Kane to be killed, after you'd all put your boots into them, and after you'd killed five nationalists,' one of the bigger men who'd run from the pavilion and knocked him down said; 'well now your number's come up, like that big squaddie your mate, and like Captain Portway. You're going to be wishing you'd never heard of Ireland, let alone been there in a fucking uniform.'

He heard a man go down some steps into what must be into a cellar.

'These are more like it,' the man said coming back.

He felt the barrel of a bigger weapon than the pistol pushed hard into the side of his neck.

'You should know the damage these can do,' the voice said. 'They're British army issue. There's two of us looking after you, and we've one apiece.'

'I'll be back with Liam and Theresa,' the man who'd had the pistol and was still behind him said. 'Liam won't want you to do too much till we're all here.'

'We might soften him up a bit, eh, soldier-boy.'

A heavy kick in the side with the sole of a boot knocked Steve off the chair, leaving him gasping and winded on floor matting, imagining what was to come.

He lay on the floor, alone with the two men who'd run from behind the pavilion and flattened down. He heard a door open. A lavatory flushed. A door closed.

'Christ, it's dark in that bog by the back door,' one of the men said. 'It needs a proper light and in the yard too. There's something just gives off a glow. I could hardly find my dick.'

'As long as your tarts can find it,' the voice of the man who'd kicked him said.

'No problem.'

Silence.

'Pat was good with the gun, pushing it into the head of this bastard,' the man that had been outside said.

'Yeah, he wants to be back in with us again, impress Liam.'

'Forget Portway, become as hard and cold as Theresa.'

'Has to. What is he without the IRA? Nothing, never was.'

Still on the floor Steve suddenly heard himself saying, 'I'm desperate for a crap. If you've done any running, you'll know it can loosen you up.'

'Fuck you having a crap,' the man who kicked him said. 'You stay on that floor till we're ready. Then your only crap will be what we beat out of you.'

'Things could be messy before that,' Steve said.

'He better go,' the other man said. 'I'll be there with my gun, like with the captain. He's hooded. He's manacled. What can he do? Fuck it. I'd like to see him try. One in the knee cap for certain, if he does.'

'Not in that bog by the back door. You've just said how pitch black it is. He could cause all sorts of trouble in that dark. We could lose him in the fucking yard.'

'No outside. Upstairs. Come on, soldier boy. And remember, I'm right behind you going up the stairs. The safety's off, so I'm ready to shoot your dangling bollocks off.'

The muzzle of a weapon was thrust under his left shoulder and into his chest. He levered himself up and began to shuffle forwards, bowed by the manacles. Raps at the side of his head from the barrel steered him to the foot of the stairs. When he reached the top, he was pushed backwards through a doorway till he felt a lavatory pan against the back of his legs.

'Manage as best you can,' the man said. 'I'll half close the door, but I'm just the other side.'

He sat on the lavatory without lowering his tracksuit bottoms. He knew the hood was not fastened too tightly at the back and that he could bow himself forward so that his hands could yank it off. They'll kill me, maybe to-night, he thought, and hurt me a lot first. If I want to see tomorrow and Helena again, it really is me or them, kill or be killed.

He pulled the hood off, worked the flush with his elbow, and then tensed himself to spring. The man pushed the door open, his gun slightly lowered.

Seeing Steve's head, he began to say 'Bast... !', as Steve, thrusting upwards with all the strength of his legs, smashed the front of his skull into the man's face, knocking him across the landing, where he hit the wall with the back of his head and crumpled unconscious, dropping his weapon. Hearing the other man running towards the stairs, Steve scrambled for the gun and, using it one handed, with the butt under his arm, blasted the man's head as it rose through the banister rails. Blood, bone and tissue spurted onto the stair-case wall in a fanning pattern, as the man was knocked back downwards. Then Steve turned again to the man on the landing, putting a round into his head before feeling for the pulse to make sure he was dead.

Blood from the gash in his forehead ran over his nose and onto his sweatshirt. I need stitches, he thought, determinedly resisting the pain and dizziness, and lifting his arm to press it on the wound. He was sure none of his blood had dripped onto the floor, and he knew he hadn't left a print on anything since he'd been in the house. Already he was planning to escape and leave no trace. Be far away with Helena - at Rocky Mountains University, Colorado!

He went down the stairs, sure that if either of the two men had the key to his manacles it would be the one he killed first. He was twisted on his back, with what was left of his head resting in a spreading pool of blood dripping down the treads. Going through his pockets, Steve thought of his dad's tales of emptying comrades' pockets in the desert in North Africa and remembered he'd done his own share of bringing in the dead in the Falklands.

These two were enemies, weren't they, like the Germans and the Argies? Finding the key and his watch, he unlocked his chains, dropping them onto the man's chest. Fastening his watch back on his wrist, he then he put the key with his house key in the pocket of his tracksuit bottoms.

Taking off his sweatshirt and T-shirt, he put the sweatshirt back on and rolled the T-shirt into a bandage to knot round his head. Picking up the two weapons, he went back down the hall into the kitchen. The photograph was on a table. He rolled it up and shoved it down the elastic waist of his track suit bottoms. Then he went outside through the front door, illuminated by an entrance light.

They'd intended to kill him. Now he'd kill them. Finish this thing once and for all. Leave a mystery behind. Get away in their Land Rover to some road signs telling him where he was. They'd killed Portway because of the O'Kanes, and they killed Yatesy because of the O'Kanes. He must stop them now, or the O'Kanes would unravel forever, and all the loose ends would always lead to him. Even far away in the States with Helena there'd be no peace.

Inside would be tricky; better stay outside; attack them, when they come to the front door.

To his right, he made out the drive. After about thirty yards it disappeared down the side of the house, but there was a path from the drive along the front of the house to the front door. Chances were, when they came back, they'd park in the drive again and walk along this path to the door. All he had to do was to hide to his left at the other side of the garden. Finding a fir-tree, very wide at the bottom, he lay partly behind it on his stomach and trained one of the weapons across the front of the house. Fifteen yards - miss at that range he deserved to be fucked.

By the time the Land Rover came back he was cold, and lying on his hands inside his sweatshirt to keep them warm. Three people, one of them a girl, climbed out and walked in a line along the narrow path to the door. Just as the first was about to reach the door, he squeezed the trigger, raking the automatic from right to left and back as he shot into their upper bodies.

'O, sweet Jesus!'

'Shite!'

Running to the Land Rover, he attacked the two men from a different direction from his firing position. They were crawling away, reaching into pockets, and he shot them in the back of the head. Then he turned to the girl who lay dying. The light above the door fell on a small, pale white face about the size of his palm and surrounded by curly hair.

Fucking hell! It was the girl from the cathedral, the girl on the walk and in the scrap yard! Blood was draining from the corner of her mouth.

'You ...!' she whispered.

'I'm sorry,' he answered, feeling strangely intimate with her.

Then another connection! The driver of the Land Rover with the ignition key still in his hand was the ginger-haired bloke who'd been on the walk with the girl, the bloke whose ankle he'd bandaged. What did all this mean?

No time to think about it now. Picking up the other gun from where he'd left it at the fir tree, he climbed into the Land Rover, started the engine, backed out of the drive, and drove off in the direction the Land Rover had just come from.

XXII

After six miles he passed a big farmhouse, a cluster of cottages, and a country pub. He didn't recognise any of them, but in another two miles there was a junction with a bigger road and a sign pointing to Ashford. Suddenly he realised he was on the Romney Marsh. No problem getting home from here.

Signs in Ashford directed him to Canterbury and, nearing Canterbury, he turned up into Chartham Hatch, ditching the guns a mile apart in woods at the side of the road. This was regular running territory which would take him back through Harbledown and across Harbledown Common to his house. Soon he drove the Land Rover from the road deeper into the woods. Switching off the engine and wiping down with a duster from the door pocket everything he'd touched, he climbed out, hurled the ignition key, the manacle key, and the ammunition clips away, tore up the photograph to scatter it in tiny pieces, and then staggered into a jog.

It took him about twenty-five minutes to reach his house. Letting himself in, he immediately undressed behind his closed door, dropping all his clothes onto the doormat. Then he had a shower, making sure he didn't break the congealed blood in the gash on his forehead. When he was dry, he bandaged the wound with dressings brought home from the sports centre's supplies. His face was swollen, and he felt an ache in his head and a pain below the ribs where he'd been kicked. He put on a clean tracksuit and a ski-cap.

He drank some coffee, ate some currant buns and a couple of bananas, and then with a bag packed, and with each item of the stuff on the doormat put into separate plastic shopping bags with their handles tied together, locked the house, backed his car off the short drive, and set off for Lancashire and his parents. It was nearly two o'clock Saturday morning. Soon he'd be far away from the five dead bodies, as if he'd nothing to do with them, as if they didn't exist. He could stay with his parents till it was time for Yatesy's funeral. He'd been due up there anyway to see his dad. He wasn't needed at the sports centre, ever again. He'd handed in all his keys and received his final salary slip and letter of severance yesterday afternoon. On the M1 and M6 he'd drop the clothes he'd been wearing into waste bins at different service stations. Even his running shoes would be miles apart.

Knowing she'd be up, even at seven in the morning, he phoned his mother from the last of the service stations to say he was on his way, but at the sight of him, her first questions were, 'Stephen, what's happened to your head? Are you in any trouble?'

'What this?' pointing to the bandage. 'I had to separate two body builders jealous of each other. Like two bull elephants. One of them nutted me, on my last day! I'll need some stitches. It's turned out worse than I thought.'

'I can see through the bandage it wants stitching, and I've not passed all your first aid exams. Are you sure you've not been in a real fight? You've been through such a lot lately with poor Yatesy, and Helena off in America. I wish we'd had chance to see her.'

'You will some day, love. I'm sure we'll come back for Christmas. For now I just want a break till Yatesy's funeral, and I wanted to see dad. Make me a cup of tea and let me go to bed for a bit. When I wake up, I'll go to Casualty.'

But lying once more in his dad's childhood bedroom, exhaustion pressing him into the bed, the reality of what he'd done, only a few hours ago, invaded his mind. He'd killed five people, giving three of them no chance. Could he go to jail for it? No Helena then! And even if he got away with it scot-free, he'd be living all his life with a terrible secret; talking to Helena, his family, friends, as if he was just like them, when he wasn't. People were just about OK with him killing as a soldier, but gunning people down like that - that girl looking into his face, as she died in the dark; as if she knew him, as if she wanted to be friends. More than the Falklands, it set him apart forever. His life, which he'd always wanted to be so straight, would become one lie after another. Couldn't he have reached the police, after he shot the first two, tell them the terrorists had hunted him, just like they hunted Yatesy? The police might have had time to ambush the rest of them at that house. Too late now.

Did killing them all appeal to him, because he really was a violent man? Or did he keep finding himself where violence had to happen, if he was to survive, and if others were to survive? He'd never wanted to live on the edge of life and death. He'd wanted to play for a great football club, but apart from that he wanted nothing unusual and was always ready to work his balls off. But it was as if he was trapped within himself - except when he was with Helena. Oh, if he could touch her now.

What did she say about the loaded gun?

Why was Mrs Thatcher screaming, 'I fight and fight and fight'?

She was at Wembley, in the middle of the pitch, spinning round on the rostrum, where the man in the white suit used to lead the community singing ('Abide with me'), when you all watched the game on telly, and your whole town was deserted till the match finished. The packed crowd was chanting 'Mag-GIE, Mag-GIE, Mag-GIE,' punching the air with clenched fists in time to the last syllable. In one corner of the stadium men, women, and children, all in miners' helmets, were trying angrily to climb over the barriers and attack her, but police and soldiers clubbed them back. A player in Argentinian strip, with a bayonet wound bleeding from his right side, lay dying at the edge of the pitch. Stan Cummings, United's assistant manager, was gently soothing the player's face with a damp sponge. The player was Ossie Ardiles.

166

He woke at one o'clock. A look in the mirror told him he must have the gash in his head stitched right away. He looked in on his dad, but he'd gone back to sleep. Then, while he was having a cup of tea and something to eat, there was a newsflash on TV. Bodies had been discovered at a house on the Romney Marsh in Kent. A lorry driver high in his cab had noticed the three lying outside. As the incident became a top story, discreet long-shots of the house revealed these bodies covered in blankets. All this was on his parents' TV, which was switched on all day to keep his mother company, but it was real and not a film, even though there was no shot of the bodies in the later reports. Instead a chief inspector faced cameras and fended off reporters.

'The investigation was only just beginning,' he said.

'Was it a feud between different wings of the IRA?'

'No comment.'

'Was it connected with the car bomb near Canterbury that killed the ex-para?'

'All lines of inquiry have just been opened.'

'Was it done by British soldiers carrying out a shoot-to-kill policy, as an IRA spokesman's claiming from Belfast?'

'No comment, gentlemen, except to say the identities of the dead bodies have not even been established as yet.'

'You're not asking us to believe they're not Irish!' someone yelled incredulously from the invisible pack.

'Isn't Kent supposed to be the "Garden of England"?' Steve's mother said. 'First poor Yatesy, then you look as if you've been in a dance hall fight, and now this. You should come back up here, where we can look after you.'

'Killings can happen anywhere,' he answered. 'If it's to do with terrorism, the whole country's full of targets.'

'There'd be no killings if people only knew how cruel it was to lose somebody you love.'

He held her in his arms, feeling again the resistance she'd always given to an embrace. Even when his dad put an arm around her for a photograph, you could see her pulling away. But now she knew her husband was dying.

'Nobody could look after dad better,' he said.

'I'll miss him,' she said.

He drove to Casualty at the local hospital and was eventually seen by a nurse in her early twenties, her uniform and belt showing her body curving in and out at all the right places.

'I'm just getting ready for the Saturday football injuries,' she said. 'All the local heroes who think they're Bryan Robson. Later it's the pub fights.'

He sat on the side of a bed, while she stood facing him, applying swabs to the gash, preparing it for stitches. The bed was curtained off. He put his hands on her hips.

'Please let me do this,' he said.

'We're not in a "Carry On" film, you know. But I'll consider it as part of the treatment. Just rest them there. Before you try anything further, remember I can cause you a lot of pain.'

'I'm Steve.'

'I know. I read the form. My name's Clare, the same as on my badge. You're not from round here, are you?'

'I use to be. My mother lives in Sycamore Road, but there's no sycamores.'

'My brother and his wife live there. Is your mother the old lady at the end terrace whose husband's in a bad way? She's three doors down from our Martin.'

'That'll be her.'

'Well, fancy that.'

'My girl-friend's a professor at a university in America. She's called Helena. I'm joining her soon. But for you I'd have a scar so terrible she might send me straight back.'

'It could have become very nasty without stitches, but you'll live. You'll soon be as good as new for her.'

He knew Helena was visiting a friend in Seattle and wouldn't be back in Colorado till late Sunday. They'd arranged he would phone her Monday evening, UK time. For the rest of Saturday he could hide away and visit his brother and sister tomorrow. It made it easier his dad couldn't take much interest in him.

That night another dream. He was playing in United's first team and had just run back on from the dressing room with his head stitched and bandaged. Sixty thousand roared for him, and 'Burnsy', the England centre half, gave him a matey whack on the shoulder as they stood together again. They were playing as if partnered for years: total dominance in the air and on the deck, his injury happening when he headed a goal from a set-piece. The crowd could see he jumped knowing he would hurt himself against their centre-back, and he saw himself going up and clashing heads and scoring, as if he was simultaneously watching the game on telly and playing. Best of all he kept releasing Alex with long diagonal balls from right to left. He saw Alex scoring twice from these passes, then, his blond hair bouncing, run back half the length of the pitch to jump into his arms, wrap his legs around his waist and kiss him. All of a sudden their right back went crazy. As another diagonal ball from Steve dropped over his head into Alex's stride, he jumped with both feet onto the back of Alex's left knee, bringing him down like a bird with a broken wing. Straight away there was fighting all over the pitch and in the crowd; nothing to do with which team anybody played for or supported - him and 'Burnsy' at each other like mad dogs! It snapped him out of his dream, and he couldn't get back into it to see how bad Alex was hurt, or how the match ended.

XXIII

Nine o'clock Sunday morning the front doorbell rang. Opening the door, Steve looked into the strangely smiling face of a short man about his own age. He was wearing an Aston Villa bob-cap and an expensive leather jacket. Very sharp side burns emerged from the bob-cap. In his left hand he held up a transparent plastic bag, an evidence bag. Inside, with the supermarket shopping bags they'd been wrapped in, were the running shoes Steve had dumped sixty miles apart on the M1. Placing this evidence bag on the ground, the man slid from beneath his leather jacket a copy of the photograph of Steve, Yatesy, the O'Kanes, and Portway. This photograph too had a transparent cover. As the man showed it to him, Steve was aware of the man looking at the wound on his forehead as if it confirmed what the man already knew.

'Rick McKnight, MI5,' the man said, holding out his hand. 'Forget this hat. I picked it up in the Midlands. I'm going to show you my credentials, and then I'm sure, Steve, you'll agree we need to talk, especially about that spectacular job you did the other night on that IRA team. What an operator! You've saved the taxpayer a helluva lot of money. We're in your debt already.'

Letting this sink into Steve, and still strangely smiling, he went on encouragingly, 'I hope that gash in your head isn't too painful. Still, any of those Irish bastards would exchange it for what you gave them.'

Steve turned round to make sure if his mother was still in the kitchen at the back of the house. He didn't want her hearing this. He didn't want anybody hearing this. He put his finger to his lips to suggest the man should keep his voice down.

'I'm here to tell you we might be able to use your talents,' McKnight continued, his voice quieter, as Steve hardly glanced at the ID and another document that had been thrust into his hand. 'It's your chance to come in from the cold; your only chance.'

'But I can't talk about any of this here.'

'No problem. But we do need to sort you out today. We have to contain that business at that farmhouse on the Romney Marsh, and we need you safe, so our story becomes the only story in town. You've seen the news.'

'What are you suggesting?'

'Are we going to sort it out here and now? I'm happy if you are. We need you with us today.'

'Today!'

'This morning, I'm telling you. We need you safe.' He paused, as if to let this sink in. Then he continued, 'OK. Put it another way. We could throw you to the wolves. Crazy soldier, out for revenge against the team that killed his army mate. You'll be all over the media; all set up for the IRA. Everybody will have you by the balls. We want to save you from all that.'

'Who's that at the door, Stephen?' It was his mother.

'It's some fella wants to talk about my car.' He motioned to McKnight that they should walk down the path to the front gate.

There he saw the Peugeot 404 McKnight must have come in. It was parked several houses away. A man sat at the wheel.

'That's Adrian,' McKnight said. 'You should see him drive. That car's not half as powerful as yours, but he'd beat you round any circuit.'

'What is it you want?' Steve asked again, feeling everything closing in on him.

'We have a safe house in the Cotswolds we want you to come to, maybe just for today, perhaps for a couple of days. I want you to meet a very senior man. We'd like you there by mid-afternoon at the latest. Drive down in your car. I'll be with you. I'd love a trip in that Jag.'

Steve not responding, McKnight continued, 'Here's another thing; what about returning to Helena in America in one piece? Nobody knows better than you she's more than worth it for any man; that body!'

'How …?'

'How do I know her?' Smiling again, McKnight tapped the side of his nose with his right forefinger. 'I've shaken hands with her - and her father, the professor. Want me to describe him - bit of a bend in his back?'

I'm really fucked, Steve thought. How long have they been on to me? How have they met Helena? Does she know about them? Is she hiding something from me? Is Charles Furlow involved after all, and even Helena's father? Is there anybody I can trust? McKnight might be lying about knowing Helena, but he can have me thrown to the wolves, all right, and destroy us both - easy.

'I can be ready by eleven,' he heard himself say.

'Good man,' McKnight answered, putting a hand on his shoulder as if bringing him into custody. 'Look, Adrian and I will go to a café I noticed. We'll be back at eleven.'

Steve told his mother there was something urgent he needed to sort out at the sports centre, before he left for good. Something he'd forgotten about. He'd been thinking about it all night.

'But you haven't seen your brother and sister,' his mother said. 'They're worried about you.'

'It's not been easy, but I really am OK. My whole life's still in front of me. I'll come up again and see you all before I finally leave. But now I need to make a phone call.'

He phoned Helena's father.

'Peter, please contact Charles Furlow again. I'm at my parents' house in Lancashire. There's a man called Rick McKnight here. He claims he's from MI5. He's coming back for me. He says he knows you, and Helena.'

'Knows me! I've never heard of any such man. Give me your number. I'll get back to you.'

He phoned at twenty to eleven.

'I've just had a very troubling conversation with Charles. In forty years of friendship I cannot remember him ever being so distant with me. He made it very clear to me that I was involving myself in things that were none of my business. I feel very offended. But he confirms Rick McKnight is an MI5 official. He said McKnight would be bald and very exactingly shaved, with sideburns. He reminded me that Helena and I once bumped into McKnight in Trafalgar Square, when we were with Charles himself.'

McKnight appeared promptly at eleven, and Steve and he were soon driving south on the M6. In the rear-view mirror Steve could see Adrian in the Peugeot, but then a Vauxhall swept in front of the Jag.

'That's Tony in that Vauxhall,' McKnight said. 'Follow it. You'll meet Tony at our destination.'

Having said this, McKnight reclined his seat and closed his eyes, his face relaxing into what seemed a natural scowl, as if things were never as well with him as he pretended. As soon as they were on the motorway he'd removed his bob-cap. It was to hide his bald-head from my mum's neighbours, Steve thought, remembering how Helena used to lie back in that seat.

In the Cotswolds they drove through the main street of Moreton-in-Marsh. Four miles further on they turned left, down a long, unmetalled road to an isolated house. They were there by three o'clock.

'Look around,' McKnight invited Steve, when they were all inside the house. 'But not the middle room.'

This was a room with a closed door that you passed on your way from the front room to the dining-kitchen, which had a pine table at its centre. You entered the front room directly from outside, dodging a row of coat pegs, on one of which McKnight had carefully hung his leather jacket. Upstairs were three bedrooms, six single beds with sleeping bags, and a bathroom. But what Steve noticed especially was that all the windows and the front and back doors leading outside were locked with very high quality security locks. Every window was also triple-glazed with the kind of strengthened glass he recognised from windows in the sports centre.

This is a prison, he thought. I'm trapped again, forty-eight hours after the IRA grabbed me. Looking out from a front landing window at his Jag, jammed front and back between the two other cars, he saw there was no chance of getting away in it, even if he could escape from the house. What are these people going to do with me, he wondered. How will they ever allow me to be with Helena.

'Whisky? Beer?' McKnight asked him, appearing from the middle room, as Steve made his way back into the kitchen. 'I've been trying for over half-an-hour to contact someone very senior on your behalf. And, by the way, you'll have to cook for us this evening.'

'Me?' Steve responded.

'Yeah you. You see we know all about you. You'll find all sorts of stuff in freezer. Have a look.'

But unable to stay still, Steve, sampling his neat, triple whisky, again moved out of the kitchen, always aware that either one of Adrian and Tony, the two drivers who'd sandwiched his Jag on the drive down, was keeping an eye on him. Passing the closed door of the middle room, where McKnight had immediately retreated with his own whisky, he heard McKnight yelling into a phone, 'Get me Minter, for Christ's sake.'

Moreton-in-Marsh, only four miles away, Steve thought. I could run there, if I could get away. I wouldn't even need the Jag.

He'd been in the house well over an hour, enough time to conclude that accepting McKnight's custody had been a big mistake, because McKnight would use him only for MI5's benefit, never for the benefit of Helena and himself. Why hadn't he gone to the police as soon as he arrived at his parents' house in Atherstone, he asked himself. He should have told the police everything, starting with the O'Kanes. His confession wouldn't have got him back to Helena straight away; but with more cover-up and lies the two of them had no chance of a life together.

Draining his whisky, he went upstairs to the bathroom. Remembering how his escape from the house on the Romney Marsh had started, he became more aware of the tightness of the stitches closing the gash in his forehead, and the ache in his ribs from when the IRA man had booted him from the chair. Omens, he thought. Good, or bad?

Staring again through the front landing window on his way downstairs, he visualised himself running into a crowded pub on the main street in Moreton-in-Marsh, yelling to everybody in the bar that he needed to talk to the police.

Could he take the three of them on, and escape?

No problem, if Yatesy was with him.

But on his own, without a weapon?

Unless he went into the kitchen, pretending to think about the cooking, and found a kitchen-knife. Then he could threaten them with a fight like a bayonet fight, like a fight in an Argy trench. They wouldn't be up for that. Nobody would who'd never done it.

Leaving his empty whisky glass on the landing window sill, he moved swiftly down the staircase.

Too swiftly, too determinedly; alarming Adrian, who was coming from the kitchen to find him.

Face to face with Adrian, Steve hit him hard at the side of the jaw with a swinging left, just like he'd once seen a night-club bouncer flatten a brawling punter.

The punch knocked Adrian down and backwards into the kitchen against the table, causing the bottle of whisky, tin tray, and extra glasses to crash from the table onto the tiled floor.

Yelling out, 'Rick, Tony,' Adrian grappled Steve around the legs, biting into Steve's thighs, as Steve kicked and punched himself free, so he could get across to the kitchen drawers, where he was sure there would be knives.

But breaking from Adrian, Steve had Tony on his back, locking an arm around his throat to throttle him. Only as Steve smashed his head backwards into Tony's face was the lock-hold loosened, allowing Steve to wrench the arm from around his throat, and then turn and kick Tony as hard as he could between the legs, dropping Tony onto his knees in sickened agony.

At the kitchen drawers Steve snatched them open till he found the knives. Spinning round, he held a knife with a nine-inch blade, like a sword.

Across the kitchen he looked straight at McKnight calmly blocking the doorway into the front of the house. Legs braced apart, McKnight's two out-stretched hands were holding an automatic pistol at chest height, and the pistol was aimed at Steve.

'What the fuck are you up to Steve?' McKnight challenged, ignoring the groans of Adrian and Tony.

'I want out,' Steve threatened. 'I want to go to the police and tell the truth.'

'We can't let you do that, Steve,' McKnight replied, still calm. 'No good will come of it for us, and no good will come of it for you and Helena. Once the US Government knows what you've done, you'll never get into the States, so bye-bye Helena. And even if you did make it over there, you'd have IRA sympathisers queuing up to kill you, all of them legally armed under the Constitution.'

'I'll take my chances. Let me out of this house.'

'No way. Look, you're all wound up. Why don't you cool down, have another whisky, shake hands with Adrian and Tony? I've told you. I'm lining up a very important man to meet you.'

'And I'm telling you I want out.'

Grabbing Tony by the hair, Steve pulled him to his feet. Blood still dripping from his broken nose, and wanting only to moan, crouch over, and nurse his balls, Tony could hardly stand.

But held by his hair, and with a knife at his throat, Tony was Steve's shield.

From behind him, Steve announced to McKnight, 'I'm coming. You have the key. Go backwards to the front door, open it, let me out, and then I release Tony. Do this, or I cut his throat.'

'Rick,' Tony pleaded, as Adrian, also alarmed, pushed himself to his feet.

'I'll kill you, Steve, before you kill Tony,' McKnight said, rocking on his feet to brace himself again, and raising the gun to take careful aim. 'Don't think I won't. And think on. No Helena, when you're dead. Some Yank will be inside her, as soon as you're inside your coffin.'

Pushing Tony in front of him, Steve moved towards McKnight, the point of the knife pressing into Tony's neck.

'Drop that knife, Steve,' McKnight said, when they were about a metre apart.

'You'll have to shoot me,' Steve said, increasing the pressure on the knife, Tony gasping 'Ah...'

'I'm all ready to do that.'

But thrusting Tony aside, Steve lunged at McKnight, knocking him to the floor, the two of them tangling in a vicious struggle, McKnight underneath Steve trying to free the gun, as Adrian, jumping on Steve's back, applied another arm lock to Steve's neck, and Tony, crouching alongside, began kicking Steve in the ribs, just where the IRA man had booted him only two days ago.

Holding McKnight down with his left hand, ignoring the terrible pain from his breaking ribs, the knife still in his right hand, Steve hit at Adrian with his right elbow. But then McKnight had the pistol to Steve's left temple, and everybody was still.

'What's it going to be, Steve?' McKnight gasped.

'Nothing you want,' Steve gasped back, knowing he was at the end of all of his strength, knowing he had no more to offer, knowing he was finished.

'Your choice, then, and this can be for Theresa O'Gara,' were the last words Steve ever heard, even while he was trying to say, 'Helena, I ...'

XXIV

'I'll come in with you,' Jan said to Helena

They were at the mortuary at Kent and Canterbury Hospital in Canterbury. Jan had phoned Helena in Colorado and met her at Heathrow with a taxi.

Helena nodded, still hoping she might waken from a nightmare, hardly believing she was back in Canterbury. Just hours ago she'd been teaching in Colorado, laughing with her students over Mark Twain. If this was Canterbury, where was Steve?

But there would never again be Steve. There was just his figure covered to the neck in sheeting, with bandages concealing terrible damage to his head. He was lying so still, so helpless, so unreachable. Nothing, not a single word she had ever read, had prepared her for such a moment as this, so she was only relieved Jan remained silent, simply letting herself be clung to as the sobbing began.

Gordon, Steve's brother, had already been down from Lancashire to identify the body.

'He's broken-hearted,' Jan said. 'He'll be coming back. He wants to meet you to discuss the funeral. He thinks it better be in the North. He's like Steve, very organised.'

Helena learned Gordon had driven down on Monday morning when Steve's body had been found in woods near Canterbury by a retired couple walking their dogs. It was lying just off a track, exposed so it could be found and identified. The woods were immediately beyond the sports centre, where she and Steve used to run together, but already the media were saying Steve hadn't been killed where his body was found.

The first in a maelstrom of claims.

It was followed immediately by the story that Steve had set out deliberately to eliminate the IRA unit which had murdered Joe Yates, and that, after his mission was completed, he had then been assassinated himself by another IRA squad.

No-one was able to source this self-propagating story, but even its gaps kept it alive.

Hours on TV and radio, and columns of newsprint, were filled insisting there was no forensic evidence that Steve had been at the house where the five bodies were found; or that these were members of the IRA cell which had murdered Joe Yates; or that Steve could have known its members were Joe Yates's killers, if they were; or that Steve himself had been eliminated by the IRA.

Alongside this story was the assertion that Steve had run into the hands of an IRA cell secluded in Kent for the opportunistic purpose of murdering an ex-soldier or ex-soldiers, especially those who'd served in Northern Ireland; that after the 'success' of its killing of Joe Yates the cell was primed for another assassination and might already have targeted Steve, who made it easy for them by persisting in jogging alone. Captured, he'd heroically escaped, using his para training and experience, and, in the words of a tabloid 'standing tall in Steve Wilson's corner,' 'given IRA cowards what they always deserve.'

A national game of speculation, similar to ones Helena recognised she'd played in the past involving public figures and tangled events - except now, in the days she remained in England till Steve's funeral, it was playing in the chambers of her heart.

'STEVEY GIRLFRIEND RIFT,' screamed the tabloid standing in Steve's corner, as it turned its unrelenting gaze on her.

Beneath the headline was a photograph in which she was shielding her face and looking furtive, as she ran into her father's house precisely to escape the photographers.

Under a sub-heading, 'Feminist Disarmer!' the tabloid detailed accurately (which woman had it bribed?) her nights at Greenham Common sleeping in a tent with other women.

Another sub-heading, 'Kinnock Comrade!' broadcast her membership of the Labour Party and support for the miners.

Reporting 'a Downing Street spokesman's confirmation' that Mrs Thatcher recognised 'Falklands Vet Steve Wilson' as 'One of her Boys', the tabloid speculated that 'Helena Edwards strung him along, before dumping him to go to America'. Sickening sexual innuendos about middle-class academic women and super-fit working-class men laced these inventions, which were soon developed by another tabloid all too eager to exploit an angle it had missed. It published a photograph of her and her happily-married cousin, taken as they walked together in Oxford, as if he were already another lover, 'with Helena Edwards' kind of education', waiting in the wings.

'If Steve Wilson's cover was blown by the murder of his friend, Joe Yates,' a radical left-wing journalist asked, 'whose agent was he, or whose had he been? Who killed him, and who actually killed Joe Yates, since no one has admitted responsibility for the car bomb?'

Major Portway was back on television and in all newspapers, demanding an inquiry into both his son's disappearance and possible connections with Steve's death. To his and his wife's horror another unknown source revealed Captain Portway was gay. Two ex-guardsmen, now openly gay, supported the claim, and rumours suggested the captain's body might be lying hidden somewhere, a fatal victim of gay-bashing.

The 'Beatrice' page really came into its own, interviewing a retired CID officer, who had particular knowledge of this crime. Under the sub-heading 'Blood-Lust', his recollections were graphic: men murdered and sometimes mutilated in cars, beds, showers.

Before this story broke, Major Portway contacted her directly to form a pressure group.

'Try to overturn some stones in the MOD and the Northern Ireland Office; see what's underneath; see if we can find answers to mysteries over there and over here.'

But she declined to join his campaign, knowing instinctively that additional public exposure would overwhelm her. How could she bear a frenzied media hunt along a trail that would connect Steve, Joe Yates, the O'Kanes, and Captain Portway? Rejecting Major and Mrs Portway, however, involved her in the haunting cover-up of Steve marching the O'Kane brothers into their son's custody. Humiliatingly, she was discovering that becoming personally untrue might be as compelling as the subterfuge of any government,

If Steve had killed the five IRA members in the house, she decided it must have been because they had captured him and threatened his life. He wasn't a calculating killer, even to avenge Yatesy. Why such events had centred on him, and therefore implicated her, she didn't know. In the aftermath of what had happened she was beginning to suspect that all her knowledge was abstract, 'in her head,' as Steve used to say; disconnected from whatever was reality.

Yet her thoughts about the Dickinson poem had become a terrible personal reality for them both. A loaded gun had been mysteriously waiting for them after all; the course of life and death directing them towards appalling, fatal collisions they could no more have anticipated than a car crashing towards them on the wrong side of a motorway.

Not that the media could have any interest in unappeasable Fate. They had too much space to fill, too many commentators living only to be heard on any and every issue, even if it was simply to brand Steve, 'A foreboding embodiment of Thatcherism'.

Joe Yates's funeral was still delayed, but Steve's body was released surprisingly quickly for the cremation. She stayed with her father at of one of his academic friends in Didsbury, east of Manchester. There, in all her father's conversation with his friend and with herself, she was aware again, as she had been ever since her return from the States, that he was apparently troubled by something more than the sheer horror of Steve's death, though she couldn't begin to think what that something more might be. He embraced and kissed her every day, as if he was bearing an unrelievable guilt.

Gordon and she had decided there was to be nothing religious in the funeral. Before it took place, he arranged for her to see Mrs Harris, his mother's neighbour, and the nurse, Clare Jones.

Looking through her window, Mrs Harris had seen a man ('he was only little') talking to Steve, and then watched him come back and drive away with Steve in Steve's car. She'd actually written down the number of the other car, but it led nowhere when detectives checked it out. As for Steve's beloved Jaguar, it was as if it had never existed. All this was now common knowledge, but it made a difference standing in Mrs Harris's window, moving aside the net curtain and listening to a narrative Mrs Harris was now practised at relating. This could be a shot in a movie, she thought, except Steve has left the set forever.

'Whatever caused that gash in his head I could sense something had really shaken him up.'

Walking from the hospital she was listening to Clare Jones, the last young woman to offer a caring touch to Steve while he was alive. Rightly, the tabloids proclaimed her to be 'very attractive'.

'He told me about you and about joining you in America,' Clare said sympathetically. 'He was back at his mother's house, but I could tell this wasn't the place for him any more. Something made him different - you, I suppose. I never told the tabloids this, but I let him put his hands on my hips while I attended to his wound. It was like comforting a boy. I sensed straight away it had nothing to do with sex. Anyway I don't have sex with men - something else I didn't tell the papers. How could anyone kill so good-looking a young man, no matter what he'd done? I spend every day trying to keep people alive - but the world's a cruel place.'

At Clare's flat a young woman, about twenty, opened the door, as if she'd been behind it all day, waiting for this very moment.

'This is Sally, my partner. She's from Keswick,' Clare said. 'Her family threw her out three years ago when she told them she was gay. She'd just passed her driving test. She thought that news would help the other. Now she drives a van for a delivery firm, don't you, my love! We've been together nearly two years. We're trying to work out how to make it up with her parents. I bet it would be easier if we lived in your kind of world.'

She shook hands with Sally and then, as she left, again with Clare.

'You're very beautiful,' Clare said.

Making his move two weeks ago at RMU, one of her new colleagues was the last person to say this to her.

'I'm involved with someone,' she'd replied, thankfully using this set response, as if from a phrase book.

But who or what was she involved with now? Lying in his coffin at the undertaker's, Steve seemed to have moved even further away from her. He was wearing the dark suit she'd seen hanging in his wardrobe, but hardly worn since he was interviewed for his job as director of the sports centre. His head still covered to just above the eyes, his face was a frozen mask, the coldest object her lips had ever touched, or her tears fallen on.

His family was inconsolable. Death, which was about to take Steve's father, who remained in bed surrounded by oxygen cylinders, had suddenly made another hardly bearable demand. Yet especially at this time Helena recognised the family's strength: Gordon's, his mother's and sister's, people she felt proud to have a connection with. Mike Connery, himself despairing because he had persuaded Steve to stay extra weeks in Canterbury, read a tribute followed by Gordon, and then the curtains closed on the coffin, and they were all outside with their desolation.

Seeing she needed some respite, Mike introduced her to a tall, fit, and distinguished looking man standing alone, Stan Cummings, United's former Assistant Manager.

Shaking their hands he observed sadly, 'What a waste of a young life. Stevey chose the wrong road when he joined the army. I'd a good chance lined up for him, success more or less guaranteed. All he needed was a bit of patience.' Then, as if acknowledging a mysterious acquaintance that had challenged him all his life, he said, 'Pride.'

She was flying back to Denver next day, because she had to catch up on teaching she'd missed in the two weeks she'd been away, especially her graduate course which none of her colleagues could cover. But there could be no pretence that closure was even pending. The very morning of her flight every media outlet published a photograph of Steve Wilson and Joe Yates handing Paul and James O'Kane over to Captain Guy Portway, and as soon as she dropped *The Guardian* onto the kitchen work surface at her father's the phone rang. It was Beatrice Furlow.

'Wouldn't you find it easier to put your side of the story to a former school friend and clear up all this mess? You know I have the "Beatrice" page in one of the popular Sundays. You could have it entirely to yourself next weekend.'

'Please leave me alone,' she replied, putting the phone down.

XXV

'Never pass up on a contact,' Beatrice's editor insisted, when she was wondering whether or not she should phone Helena Edwards. 'Why shouldn't she want to confess like everybody else? Who else but a free press is there to confess to?'

But Beatrice remembered Helena as one of the serious ones, still a virgin everyone thought, when she went to Oxford. In their final year at school she won the debate on Colonialism, taking an anti-imperialist stance, actually quoting from *Things Fall Apart*, a novel no-one had heard of except Jane Cassidy, the new head of English. Beatrice knew it was because of this debate that, only last week, she'd surprised a tetchy academic on *Late Hour* by actually knowing something about Achebe, even though she'd never read a word of his. At school she used to wonder if her own parents wouldn't have preferred Helena as a daughter, but putting down the phone after Helena replied, 'Leave me alone,' she thought suit yourself. Look at the relationship you got yourself into, a nobody soldier involved in an orgy of violence. How can that be better than Simon, and all that IRA stuff to embarrass daddy?

Thoughts that were to haunt her ten days later.

Fresh from the shower after a fitness session with Clarence, Brendan suddenly announced he would be moving over to their New York apartment.

'I've signed Clarence off,' he added.

'Your soul-mate! What's happened?'

'Nothing, he's still perfect. He's just taught me to walk on my hands. But I can't take him to New York, and after that it'll be California.'

'But why and when? You know I'm down for six more appearances on *Late Hour*.'

'I want to go right away. I'm feeling used up and stale, Bea. For months I've only been re-treading myself.'

'But why don't we both go later, in the New Year? I can write from anywhere, and I'd love to do some pieces on New York and LA.'

'It can't wait. I'm going to the studio and nothing's happening. Other people are queuing up to use the gear, and I'm becoming an embarrassment to my own technicians. I can see they think I'm spent.'

Then it came out, 'Well it's not been with me!'

'What does that mean?'

'Simon, look at us. Don't you ever think about our marriage? If we're not hosting parties, we're seldom in the house together, never mind in bed together.'

'Your hours are as complicated as mine.'

'It's not that. I'm beginning to think all you want from me is someone playing the part of wife. Beyond that, what's your interest in me? Why don't you want children? Isn't there going to be something more human in our lives than all this make-believe: you faking it for your bands in the studio, me saying on television and in magazines more or less the first thing that comes into my head? Is this all there is?'

'Nobody knows. But you can have a child if you want one.'

Two days later, with little more than a kiss on the cheek, he was gone on Concorde. Four days after that he phoned from California to say he was on his way 'down to Argentina.'

Then her life disintegrated.

Explosively Simon was named as a source of laundered money financing several IRA safe-houses, including the farmhouse on the Romney Marsh where all those killings had been done! TV told her this just before the police pounded on the door of Connaught Square with search warrants to crawl all over it and Wes's. Immediately a pack of reporters invaded the Square, hunting down its quarry as if she weren't one of their own! Every day on the news she saw herself pushing through a scrum of cameras and yells.

'Beatrice, will you be going over to the Argies with Simon?'

'How long's he been funding the IRA?'

'Why didn't you suspect anything?'

'Will having no children make it easier for you to divorce him?'

Only this last question, once she was safely behind the closed door, brought bitter tears into eyes that were always determinedly dry for the world outside. She spent hours 'Helping the police with their enquiries,' and assuring the media herd, 'I'm absolutely not under arrest. I know absolutely nothing about my husband's relationship with the IRA. I live here, and I intend to stay here.'

Simon's father, it turned out, was an IRA courier, hiding in the Republic.

Her own father speedily retired, only to walk into his own media storm when it was alleged MI5 had had the photo of Steve Wilson, Joe Yates, the O'Kane brothers, and Captain Guy Portway for months and ought to have prevented the killing of the soldiers and the captain, if indeed the captain was dead. Major Portway was again on all channels now proclaiming his loss of faith in national institutions he'd served all his life.

'This is all I had till the end,' her father assured her, giving her the torn photograph of the O'Kanes and Captain Portway.

'It suddenly appeared on my desk, but I couldn't discover its source, or who else knew about it. I suspected someone was setting me up. Then, the morning the car bomb went off, the soldier Joe Yates appeared in another torn version of the photograph again left mysteriously on my desk. I never saw the complete photograph including Steve Wilson, until it was published in the newspapers. You must understand I've been on the edge of things for some time.'

Beatrice could almost hear him closing the doors on his career, content to let her create whatever smokescreen she could for both of them.

'Your mother intends us to move lock, stock and barrel to France - to Provence to be precise,' he told her. 'We've always thought we might do it, and now she thinks there's nothing left for us here. As she sees it, every new year is just like the last.'

Remembering his stories to the family of how he'd been something of a star in student theatre in his Oxford days, Beatrice wondered if her father was even now playing a part. How much did he really know about the killing of Steve Wilson? What had caused the sudden rift between him and Helena Edwards' father? They'd been the closest of friends for forty years. Each had been best man at the other's wedding.

But all she said was, 'Why don't you keep a base in England, a flat somewhere? You can always stay with me, of course, but wouldn't you like a place of your own. I've plenty of money, if that's a problem.'

'Not for us,' he assured her, before sighing, 'ah, this house, the wine cellar!'

'Help yourself to whatever you want.'

She didn't mention she now had more earning power than ever. Notoriety put up her price without her asking, and everybody wanted to interview her. Her network was lining her up to front a new series of programmes entitled *Deception*.

Christmas nearing, the police finding nothing at Connaught Square or Wes's, the turmoil settled down, and the media swarmed around another story. Returning alone in the darkness to Connaught Square from a long preliminary evening session about *Deception*, she was blankly watching *Late Hour* with a glass of water in her hand, having been told by the producers of *Deception* to watch her weight.

Triumphantly *Late Hour* announced it had a tape of an unprecedented live interview with wonder guitarist Shane Webb himself, done that evening in a first class lounge at Heathrow, while Shane waited for his limousine. The TV crew, it turned out, was at the airport to interview a British film star returning from American acclaim, but Concorde was very late leaving New York, and just before take-off the film star, unbeknown to the TV crew, decided to travel the following day. Fortunately the interviewer was obsessed by contemporary music and especially by Shane.

The tape showed the interviewer approaching Shane, and his latest sensational girlfriend reverently. Immediately, all the talk was technical stuff: influences, early and later work, unusual chords, relations between chords, fingering, open tuning. For once Shane didn't seem to mind the camera. After all, what else would he do, Beatrice thought, but eat painkillers till the limo arrived?

But then the interviewer said, 'From the West coast haven't you been down to Argentina to work with Simon Gallagher?'

'What of it?'

'I just wondered how he was. I expect he's moved on. He seemed a bit stuck in London.'

'The sounds, you mean?'

'What else?'

'Yeah, we were both stuck. We've both moved on. But he's always been the best. In the studio he's a genius.'

'And outside doesn't matter?'

'Outside?' Shane seemed baffled. But then he understood, 'In the scale of things? No. Only the music can hope to matter.'

'But people were hurt, killed. Where's the justice?'

'Justice!' Shane blew air through his lips and slowly shook his head in meditative wonderment. 'When you find it, let me know.'

A uniformed chauffeur came respectfully into view, and Shane signalled that the interview was at an end. But then he had a final thing he wanted to say.

'Simon can't stand anybody being made to feel an inferior human being, Irish or me - anybody! I love him!'

The camera was still running while the chauffeur and the girlfriend eased Shane from the low easy chair to his feet, tremors of pain registering on his face. Through her tears, it seemed to Beatrice that as he rose he was trying in vain to free himself from a vicious sword pushed down through his spine by invisible hands.

XXVI

Last night, alone in bed in his apartment, Rick McKnight had again woken up sweating in panic, knowing his career was hanging by a thread, knowing he'd nearly totalled himself by killing Steve Wilson and, before that, taking Maddie to Orgreave and telling her all that stuff in bed in the hotel. What must he have been feeling for her then? What was he feeling for her now? Sure, she wasn't Maddie. She was Theresa O'Gara. She was the enemy, and he had to be glad she was silenced forever; but looking into her dead white face, as she lay on her back outside that farmhouse on Romney Marsh, there were tears in his eyes. And later, he had to turn away, when the pathologist told him the bullet, entering her right side, had smashed its way through to her heart. He wished now he'd inflicted more pain on Steve Wilson.

But he never intended to kill that crazy squaddie. He just thought he'd get him safe. Why couldn't everybody see that? And anyway the result turned out OK.

'We need this handling,' he'd heard Minter murmur, when, after the killing of Joe Yates, nearly everybody in the MI5 building suddenly had a copy (from where?) of that photograph of Portway, the O'Kanes, Joe Yates, and Steve Wilson.

So he, Rick McKnight, had set about handling it. Adrian and Tony found that IRA cell in Kent, and everything came together, Steve Wilson himself cleaning up most of it for them, and he, Rick McKnight, capturing Steve Wilson to present him to Minter.

Except when they all got to the safe house in the Cotswolds, Minter couldn't be contacted because he was at a jamboree at the American Embassy, and Steve Wilson had suddenly decided to become Rambo. Even then, he, Rick McKnight, had delivered a result. With Steve Wilson dead, he'd sown enough confusion to leave everybody with their heads up their own ass.

And before all that the TV footage of Orgreave absolutely shafted the miners, even the BBC playing better than expected; editing a sequence of events to show the miners initiating a violent attack, when they'd actually been responding to one.

What more could Minter want from him?

But though Minter smiled at him, shook his hand, there was no more Vigilance for Rick McKnight.

Instead, this December Monday morning on the way to Christmas, here he was, after another desperate night, answerable to Judith Rae. He was back in his usual chair, while she faced him from Furlow's chair and from behind Furlow's desk.

Looking across the desk at her, he remembered again the humiliation of last Friday afternoon, during the get-together called by Minter in one of the bigger conference suites. McKnight had assumed the drinks were just to oil the way to the festivities, but suddenly everybody knew Judith Rae had Furlow's job, now that Furlow had disappeared, as if he never existed. Immediately afterwards Judith Rae, her red hair newly trimmed for her promotion, was telling him, 'Rick, my new office, Furlow's old room, Monday morning, first thing.'

'Balls up is what I'm looking at here,' she was already saying to him, as he entered the room this morning and sat down to face her. 'You took a woman to Orgreave. If we ever find her ...! Then there's that police superintendent you bribed, from Essex. Didn't you notice he was about to retire? He's making out he has stuff to sell.'

Before he could offer any kind of response, she drilled into him further.

'This Kent slaughter-house is the worst thing. Two ex-paras and an IRA unit killed; MPs and journalists scavenging; the IRA feeding them juicy scraps, "Shoot to kill on the Mainland"; special branch gloating over our incompetence; Major Portway and his wife all over the media. It ain't good, especially after Brighton. David tells me you had two cowboys running loose. Well, they're silenced and gone. You need to earn your pay check, Rick.'

Only with the last word, McKnight felt, did Judith Rae show him any personal recognition. Furlow kept him at arms' length, but Furlow always knew it was him in the room. Not this bitch. Suddenly McKnight realised he'd never registered with her, despite the sessions in the Compass when, for all her blokey lingo, she always stayed sober. He was just a name on a list, a function. He wasn't even convinced she'd any real interest in the service they were both in. For her it could be any career, any operation, with a top and bottom line. If the read-out was good, who gave a toss what the business was doing?

'We're surprised,' Judith Rae went on, 'that you thought you had authority to run men on your own. From now on clear everything with me, and I mean clear. Nothing vague or casual. Put it in writing.'

Then roll it up and ram it in you, McKnight countered silently. Balls-up was right; only it was his balls Minter had put into her grip, so the two of them could have him where they wanted him, all set up to take the next fall, whenever it was needed.

She's shagging Minter, McKnight concluded for the umpteenth time since Friday, as he watched Judith Rae shuffle through some papers. Screwing their way to the top always gives women the advantage over men. That's why she got the reward of tailing Scargill to Paris in October, when Scargill met one of Colonel Gaddafi's henchmen to wangle some Libyan money for the strike. That trip was a bonus for servicing Minter.

McKnight would have shed blood for the Paris operation. Instead, when it was completed, he'd had to listen to Judith Rae celebrating in the Compass.

'Is Scargill mad, or is he mad!' she'd mocked. 'The prime-minister's always been convinced her enemies are gang-banging Britannia, and here's the leader of the National Union of Mineworkers strutting his stuff in the company of a regime supplying weapons and explosives to the IRA!'

That was the night, McKnight remembered, Judith Rae was on a high, as she is this morning; completely the wrong night for that guy with long hair to fondle her ass in her tight trousers.

Standing back to back with Judith Rae while she was buying a round at the bar, the guy was with his mates, men and women, who had seats at a table in front of him. All he did was reach behind him for a squeeze. Next thing, Judith Rae span round and wrenched the guy's right arm up his back, while her left hand clamped the back of his neck and forced the side of his face down on the table. Beer and wine spilling everywhere and washing through the guy's hair, the whole pub watched in astonishment as Judith Rae rhythmically pressured the guy's arm.

'Apologise, you crude bastard,' she said in time to the pressure. 'Say you're sorry for touching me like that. Say it all out loud, and that women must be respected. Or I'll rip your shoulder out of its socket.'

The guy, in a lot of pain, did as he was told, though it was only in a mumble; then people moved silently out of his way, as he took himself out of the pub, followed by his crying girlfriend, who'd been sitting at the table, and who had beer all down the front of her white jeans and between her legs.

Get it into your head Judith Rae's not to be messed with, and you'll be OK, McKnight now told himself, as he watched her use Furlow's keys in Furlow's key-wallet to open drawers in Furlow's old desk.

Then, when she looked up at him, as if she'd forgotten he was there, he said, 'Judith, I'm sure we'll be able to work well together as a team.'

XXVII

Helena stood with Carol in the hallway of the cottage at Restore, both of them crying, holding on to each other.

Absolute separation: Helena knew Carol also was living under that sentence till her own death. All you could hope for was the anodyne of time, that you would stop thinking about someone you didn't want to forget.

The taxi-driver hadn't forgotten Restore. When Helena stepped out of Jan's house and said its name, he nodded knowingly. Because of the murder and funeral of Joe Yates, he'd carried journalists and sightseers to this destination many times. As she paid him, he seemed also to recognise her own face from its brief life in the media, but he said nothing. Perhaps he was reserving her for his mates, or for his family when he was at home.

'People come to look at the place all the time, even though we're still closed,' Carol said when they were having a cup of tea and Carol was breast-feeding. 'If I'm outside, they try to take photos of me and the baby, don't they Joey, love? If we were open, we'd be lucky if they even bought a door-knob.'

Extensions to the cottage had been postponed, so the scaffolding was removed. But as if to live up to its name and prove life must move on, Restore was to re-open in the New Year. Carol's younger sister (already divorced) would manage the retail business. Joe's foreman was looking after the demolition side. Carol would stay in overall command.

'We have to earn our living, don't we, Joey?' Carol said.

It would need Raphael to paint how beautiful you and Joey are, Helena was thinking. Birth, she realised, was as fundamental as death, but would she ever have anything to do with birth?

'Most of the time, especially among people in the street,' she said, 'I feel invisible. It's as if I expect people to know what's happened, make some sign, even in Colorado, which I know is silly; it's as if I'm inhabiting a different reality.'

'I know what you mean,' Carol agreed, 'though it's not the same for me, living in this area, and having Joey. Our photos have been all over the local papers and regional television news. I'm recognised all the time. I see people in supermarket aisles nudging each other about me. I want that to go away.'

'We could never have thought anything like this would happen.'

'No,' Carol sighed. 'After little Joey we were going to have at least one more. I saw them all running round the yard, with me working at home and always being here for them. We thought we'd always be friends with you and Steve. Joe thought we'd come and visit you in America.'

'We would have loved that.'

'We hoped you and Steve would be permanent, as if it makes any difference now. We could see he wanted it to last.'

'I did too, as far I could think about the future. We were only just beginning our relationship.'

'I know Joe and me were more traditional,' Carol said sympathetically. Detaching Joey from her breast, she commented lovingly to him, 'You're like your daddy, filling yourself to the top.'

The dark nipple was erect and wet from Joey's sucking.

Nearly thirty years old, Helena thought, and it's the closest I've ever been to a woman breast-feeding a baby.

'Sometimes traditions are traditions because they're very valuable,' she said. 'I want to be successful in my career, but I've never seen myself as some free-lance woman, as far as men are concerned. I've always known I needed a relationship with a man, and what's any relationship worth if there's no commitment?' There were tears in her eyes again as she said, 'I'd be even more heartbroken than I am already, if Steve didn't know how much I wanted to be with him.'

Carol's eyes were also wet. 'I'm sure he did,' she said. 'And you must know how proud it made him to be with you.'

They were silent while she winded Joey and then changed him. 'Sleep and feed, feed and sleep,' she teased, tickling his tummy. Then, 'Do you want to hold him?'

'Please.'

She held Joey chest down on her breast, kissing the top of his forehead, smelling his hair, feeling his solid, compact warmth against her - someone to love.

'When do you go back to America?'

'January sixth.'

'We both make a new start in the New Year.'

'Not one we wanted.'

'No.'

'I'll come and see you again, when I come back to England. I'd like to see Joey grow up. I'm sure he'll be big and strong.'

'Yes. I have to keep going for his sake. Sometimes I can't bear to think about it - all the years stretching ahead, without his daddy, never knowing what Joe was really like.'

'We must make sure we tell him, he was a daddy to be proud of.'

'Thank-you, Helena.'

The taxi she'd arranged to take her back to the city would soon be arriving. She handed Joey back to Carol and watched her put him gently into his downstairs cradle. He yawned, stretched himself out, and went back to sleep, unaware of anything except that he was comfortable, his life waiting for him.

In the hall they held each other again.

'It's so very, very hard,' Carol said.

'I know.'

Yatesy, Steve, the O'Kanes and Portway? Obviously, Carol had seen the photograph and heard all the speculation. But Helena knew the two of them would always leave this matter deeply buried.

She also knew she would never reveal to anyone what her father had told her about Charles Furlow.

XXVIII

Back in Canterbury the taxi dropped her near St George's Roundabout. She wanted to walk through the city and visit the cathedral once more before it was time to go back to Jan's cottage, in St Dunstan's, for tea, and then catch her train to Oxford.

Two days ago, on her first morning with Jan, she'd met Steve's brother Gordon, who'd been staying with Mike and Catherine Connery. She and Gordon had gone together for a final interview with the police in Maidstone. Afterwards the senior detective had accompanied them to Gordon's car.

'Off the record, and now we're in the open air,' he said. 'I want you to know it wasn't the IRA who killed Steve Wilson. We're not fools in the police, whatever the so called intelligence people think.'

Now, walking among the Christmas shoppers along the medieval narrowness of Mercery Lane towards Christ Church Gate, Helena wondered if Steve's and Yatesy's violent deaths could ever matter to this very ancient city, which was long ago as bloodied as twentieth century Dallas by a momentous assassination in the cathedral itself, and then by later martyrdoms. Did even the truth matter? The world only ever used as much of the truth as suited it, or it had time for - sanctifying Becket and, what could amount the same thing, glamorising JFK. She herself, she had to recognise, only used the great cathedral for her own purposes, as she was doing now.

Entering by the main south door, she turned immediately down the south aisle. She was aiming for a particular memorial tablet to a soldier, one of the many decorating the cathedral walls; some commemorating battles she'd heard of, such as Waterloo; others marking conflicts she knew little about, such as Afghanistan in the eighteen thirties.

Arriving at the white marble tablet she was searching for, she noted again how it showed the right arm and upright spear of a helmeted young Britannia embracing a dying soldier. She read the words beneath this image, as she had once done with Steve.

Sacred to the Memory of Lieut Colonel JOHN STUART who fell at the Head of the 9th Regiment of Infantry, in the 32nd Year of his Age, at the Battle of Rolera, on the 17th of August, 1808, while the British Arms were successfully supporting the cause of Portugal against the Usurpation of France. ...

'I'll soon be thirty-two,' Steve had responded.

'But you came back from your battles,' she answered, squeezing his hand. Then, wanting to lead him on, 'And you were anything but detumescent.'

'What!'

'Look at the sword completing the soldier's slack right arm, as he dies into Britannia's embrace; its point on the ground, done with - spent.'

'Here we go again!'

'Don't you see the patriarchy at work here, the sentimentality, the implicit degradation of real women and their carnality? The soldier's in the swoon of death, leaving behind fallible manhood, which is always betrayed by women. He's moving into the immortal, protective embrace of virginal Britannia. No more need for messy sex and messy life. Those maidenly breasts beneath Britannia's clothing surely promise only a kind of uncorrupted solace for his soul. Forget naked Eve, who caused all the problems in the first place and will always cause more. This dying man will never again need that kind of woman. He'll never again be led astray by her. No more "Carmen Killings".'

'He's got no dangly bits,' Steve had acknowledged, indicating the soldier's smooth crotch.

'See what I mean!'

Remembering this moment, she suddenly felt her whole being at one with Steve's, hearing him say, from another occasion just before she left for the interview at RMU, 'God, I love this with you!'

It was another night in his bed. He was resting inside her, both of them blissfully embracing each other, waiting for ultimate sensation to overwhelm them.

'I love it with you too.'

'So you don't think it's a mistake, then, to love someone?'

He was challenging her with what a character says in Elizabeth Bowen's *The Death of the Heart*. She'd told him about the character earlier that afternoon, when they'd gone to photograph Bowen's house at Hythe.

'I hope you already know I don't.'

Oh, to touch herself to him, to-night, this afternoon, to hurry to his house now!

Never again.

As she sat down to dry her eyes, another woman immediately occupied the next chair. She was about her own age, but altogether better turned out - her red hair very well-cut, her coat expensive, her high heels, gloves and hand-bag all matching.

'Helena,' she said, as if they were old friends.

'Do I know you?'

'No, but that doesn't matter. After this I'll disappear from your life. What life depends on you.'

'What do you mean? Who are you?'

'It's not important who I am. What is important is what you choose to involve yourself in - talking to the police, for instance.'

She tried to stand up, but the woman put a firm hand on her shoulder, pressing her down.

'We can make it very awkward for you. You're an alien in the States. Just by mentioning Greenham Common to the right people we can mess up your visa, have you thrown out of the country. Your academic career will be terminated, over there, over here. Keep your nose out of the Steve Wilson business. He's dead. It's finished.' Pausing so this could sink in, she then continued, 'I'm going to stand up now and leave. Give me fifteen minutes before you move. Use them to think about what happened to your boyfriend.'

Gazing sightlessly towards the choir screen, Helena heard the woman's dominating high heels walk away down the aisle. Would there be violation after violation, her life endlessly invaded? She wanted only to protect her love for Steve.

XXIX

'It's nineteen eighty-four, and I feel I've done time in "Room 101",' Jan had joked tensely three days ago, when Helena arrived to stay with her. 'I don't smoke. I'm feeling fit. I'm cleansed. Why shouldn't I be acceptable?'

Recognising the miners' strike was all but lost, she was reviewing her year, asking herself if it had been futile.

'I joined the Labour Party in nineteen sixty-one, on my first day at university,' she'd announced as they settled down to a bottle of wine on that first evening. 'My tutor was an influential communist, who'd just visited Castro's Cuba. He had a large red-brick house in Leeds. Students called it the Kremlin. He invited his first years over, showed us his slides of Cuba, and told us how wonderful Cuba was and was going to be. How Castro had come down from the mountains like a messiah. None of us imagined this messiah would become a dictator, and if my tutor even recognised Stalin had murdered on an industrial scale, he implied it was the cost of changing history, even an historical inevitability. Hungary was so the Soviet Union could maintain a sphere of influence matching America's.'

Sipping her wine, she went on sadly, 'What happened to all that hope? Why hasn't the Labour Party articulated any kind of convincing case to mediate between Scargill and Thatcher? Is it because its leaders know even socialism is no more than a fantasy? Now we're all to settle for Thatcher's triumphalism, as if the tarnishing of ideals doesn't tell us something distressing about human nature, about ourselves? All we're left with is mutual exploitation. Resist, and you're "the enemy within".'

'You don't exploit,' Helena remembered replying. 'Nor do lots of other people, at least not consciously, deliberately. Whether we like it or not, we all find ourselves complicit in systems that exploit, and we have to accept no cause can be as true as we want it to be, no issue black or white. I always doubted the Falklands war, never knowing I would meet Steve. But look at the atrocities the generals were committing during their murderous regime in Argentina. Could we have left the Falklanders to that? Steve once asked me if I'd wanted us to lose.'

'I shouldn't be pouring all this onto you,' Jan responded, 'but I'm feeling so completely lost: the state of the country, three or four million unemployed - Steve and his friend horribly murdered, you leaving.'

'You've been heroic this year. You've a right to think about yourself, no one more so.'

This afternoon when she returned from the cathedral, instead of wine and cheese, it was tea and home-made scones and cherry cake.

They discussed Helena's prospects at RMU.

'"Everybody wants America; they just won't admit it",' Helena quoted. 'Do you remember Rebecca Rabinowitz saying that to us last summer on a Sunday morning walk? Now I'm employed in the States, and even my father thinks he might find something on the East coast for his final years. His books are still authoritative, and coming from Oxford counts, even though he claims he's finished with Oxford forever.'

'Rebecca never recognises the whole world can't be America,' Jan countered, 'because America needs much of it to be in a state of subservience to America, and providing for America. Hence the term "America's back-yard", used of all those supposedly independent countries south of Texas and Florida, not to speak of Middle-Eastern oil states and their friendly dictators.' She paused, and then said with a rueful smile, 'But I'd still like to visit you in the States.'

'You must.'

Eating some cake and drinking her tea, Helena then said, 'I've given Steve's family my American address.' After a few moments she added, 'I still can't believe he's dead. When the phone rings, I think it's likely to be him. Carol Yates says it's the same with her.'

'She has her baby.'

'That wasn't on the cards for us immediately, but I would never have had a termination.'

'Steve wouldn't have wanted that, not for any child of his.'

'No.'

'Even my marriage was hopeless,' Jan had once revealed to her, 'though we split up on reasonable terms. He was useless in every way, politically and around the house. In bed I might as well not have been there. Complete self-indulgence. He wanted to be some kind of hippy for the rest of his life. Earning a living was for drudges, but he thought it simple comradeship for a socialist like me to put my salary into our joint bank account.'

No wonder Jan was so interested in Steve.

'He'll do his utmost for you,' she had once said to her. 'Admirable.'

With her rucksack and light bag she was walking from Jan's house to Canterbury West Station, and she and Jan had already agreed to say good-bye in the house. Now, when their afternoon tea was finished, she went upstairs to get her stuff. Attending to her period in the loo, she was reminded again how indifferently the body continues its functions until its end comes. Emily Dickinson, she thought: parts of the self (body, mind, brain, soul) were as if separate from the self, whatever the self was. Your one and only life and death might be a loaded gun, but, as in the poem, you only knew it after the event, if you knew it at all. Beforehand you could never know what your time had waiting for you. You could only know you were going to die and hope life treated you fairly.

'Wrong time, wrong place,' a reporter had said of Steve's death, 'simple as that.'

At the half-opened front door Jan hugged her as if she couldn't be sure where another hug would come from.

'That book you're writing - about literature and places - there'll be a dedication?' Jan asked, as she dabbed her eyes with a handkerchief.

'That's already written, Helen said sadly. 'It's "In Loving Memory of Steve Wilson".'

THE END